Death by Chowdah

Shipwreck Café Mysteries
Book #1

DONNA WALO CLANCY

BOOKSMITH
MUSICSMITH

BOOKS/CDS/VINYL/DVDS&VHS
SHEET MUSIC
MUSICAL ACCESSORIES
MAGAZINES/GREETING CARDS
GIFT ITEMS/USED ITEMS
SENIOR DISCOUNT DAYS

FREQUENT BUYER'S CLUB

SPECIAL ORDERS OUR
SPECIALTY

**A locally owned independent
book and music store
serving the community**

**136 Route 6A
Orleans, MA 02653
(508) 255-4590**
booksmith.musicsmith@comcast.net

Copyright © 2017 Donna Walo Clancy

Death by Chowdah
By Donna Walo Clancy

ISBN-13 9781543111927
ISBN-10 1543111920

All Characters and events in this book are a work of fiction. Any similarities to anyone living or dead are purely coincidental. Donna Walo Clancy is identified as the sole author of this book.

All rights are reserved. No part of this publication may be reproduced, stored in a retrieval system, or transmitted in any form or by any means, except for brief quotations in printed reviews, without the prior written permission of the author.

Cover art by Melissa Ringuette at Monark Design Services
Interior by Rogena Mitchell-Jones at RMJ Manuscript Service
Edited by Debra Wagner

Cover Photos from Adobestock.com
man and golden - captblack76
lighthouse and dunes – ryszardfilipowicz

First Edition
Printed in the U.S.A.

Contents

Acknowledgments vii
Dedicated to My Readers ix
Chapter 1 1
Chapter 2 9
Chapter 3 19
Chapter 4 29
Chapter 5 38
Chapter 6 49
Chapter 7 63
Chapter 8 79
Chapter 9 86
Chapter 10 100
Chapter 11 110
Chapter 12 115
Chapter 13 124
Chapter 14 139
Chapter 15 152
Chapter 16 157
Chapter 17 174
Chapter 18 184
Chapter 19 191
RECIPES 197

Acknowledgments

Thank you, Melissa Ringuette, for another outstanding cover!
Covers are the eyes to the story held within.
I am so lucky to have you on my team.

Debra Wagner my editor:
It is so hard to find an editor that you can trust with your work.
From day one, you have been a professional in every aspect.
Thank you. I see many books heading your way.
"Your story is the diamond and I am the one who polishes it to make it shine."

Rogena Mitchell-Jones at RMJ Manuscript Service:
Thank you for the wonderful formatting job. Book release time is stressful enough without worrying that the book will load wrong. You're the best!

Recipes donated by:
Tim Daniel, Melissa Kay Clarke, Kathy Julin, Cathy MacKenzie, and Betty Studley

Dedicated to My Readers

I thank you for the encouragement to write the next one.
I thank you for the words of happiness you share with me when you enjoy my stories.

I thank you for the friendships I have made along this writing journey.

You are so appreciated.

Chapter 1

"I GUESS HE comes with the property," Jay said, looking at the skinny, disheveled dog laying on the back porch of the caretaker's cottage.

"No one knows where he came from," answered Anna Snow, his financial consultant. "Sometimes, tourists come to the Cape for vacation and leave their animals behind. Other times, the animals escape from the car or hotel and just end up lost. You could give him a home here, now that you bought the place. He's friendly, but a little skittish."

"Come here, boy," Jay crooned quietly, standing just inside the cottage door.

The dog didn't move. He warily kept his eyes on the first person who had attempted to come near him in a very long time. Jay inched closer and the dog lifted his head. The six foot one inch man sat cross-legged on the floor and extended his hand for the dog to smell.

Ever so slowly, the dog edged his nose closer to Jay's fingertips. He smelled the offered hand of friendship from a safe distance, all the while never taking his eyes off the man sitting on the floor in front of him.

"Come on. Come see me," coaxed Jay.

The dog stood up and limped his way over to his new friend. He sat in front of Jay who then reached out to pat him. The dog cringed back, like he was going to get hit. His ears went down and his head drooped.

"I think he's been abused," stated Anna, shaking her head.

"What a shame."

"You're with me now, big guy. Are you hungry?"

The dog looked at him, cocking his head. You could almost see it in his eyes that he was relieved that he hadn't been struck.

"Stay with him, Anna. I have a turkey sandwich in the car he might like. I'll be right back."

Jay disappeared out the front door. The dog never moved; he just watched intently to see if his new friend was going to come back. When the man reentered the cottage, the dog's tail started to wag. Breaking off a piece of the sandwich, Jay offered it to the underweight animal. The golden gingerly took the food offered to him, then swallowed it whole, looking for more.

Jay broke the sandwich into small pieces and set it in front of the dog, but he didn't go near the food. The fear was evident in his eyes.

"It's okay. Go ahead," he said, trying to get the dog to eat.

The dog still didn't move towards the food. Jay sat down on the floor and picked up a piece of the sandwich and held it out. The dog cautiously took the food from his hand.

"I see how it is," he said, laughing. "You want to be fed."

As hungry as the dog was, he gently took each piece that was handed to him. When the sandwich was gone, he laid down next to Jay's leg and closed his eyes in contentment. His fur was matted and it appeared that he had a bad gash on his rear paw. Jay stroked the matted fur. The dog cringed at the first touch, but relaxed the more Jay stroked him and talked to him.

"What are you going to do with him?" Anna inquired.

"First, I have to get him into my car if he'll even leave this place. Then, I need to take him to the vets and have him checked over. He probably will require vaccines, and that back paw should be attended to."

"He seems to trust you," Anna offered, smiling.

The dog rolled over on his side to get closer to Jay's leg.

"Well, now, it seems that he is a she! She can stay with me

at the cottage until I move here permanently. Then we both will have a new home together," Jay remarked.

"What are you going to call her since you don't know her name?"

"I've always wanted a dog named Buddy, but she's too pretty to be called that. She's had a rough life so far so I think the name Stormy would be perfect for her. She'll get used to the name when she has heard it often enough."

"I love it," Anna agreed, bending to pat the dog. "Hello, Stormy. Nice to meet you."

"The contractors will be here tomorrow and have promised the work should be done in four weeks for the café eating area. I have separate contractors coming in for the kitchen. I know we discussed not going over budget, but I really want to get this place open for the summer season," Jay confided, still patting the dog who had drifted off to sleep next to him.

"How much over budget are we talking about?" asked Anna, frowning.

"About fifteen thousand."

"Well, I suppose it could be worse," she stated in return.

"I'm going to move into here next week. I have professional cleaners coming in on Monday to clean the cottage from top to bottom. The water and electricity have already been turned on in all the buildings."

"Have you talked to Robbie yet?"

"No, I figured I'd wait. In a week or two I'll let him know what's happening. He still doesn't know I bought the lighthouse," answered Jay. "He'll freak out, since we used to play here when we were little kids."

Jay Hallett was thirty years old and was starting on a new path in his life. A city attorney up until three months ago, he decided to leave Boston and return to the slower lifestyle of Cape Cod. Fed up with the way the judicial system was working, or not working, in his words, he took his savings and bought the abandoned lighthouse and surrounding buildings. He had always loved to cook and so decided to turn Anchor Point Lighthouse into a café.

Six foot one, curly black hair, and bedroom blue eyes made him one hot looking guy. People told him he was a carbon copy of his Dad who had died of cancer when Jay was only ten years old. He worked out three times a week, which resulted in him having abs of steel. Running the beach was by far his favorite type of exercise. And, as a true romantic, he always knew how to treat a lady.

There was never a lack of dates while he had lived in the city. He never knew whether the women were dating him for his personality or because they were looking for a rich attorney husband. Jay decided he was going to take a step back from dating for a while and concentrate on his new business. He decided it would be all right to keep his eyes open, but not to keep up the extreme dating schedule he had while living in Boston.

His business would be his first and foremost priority until it was established. What used to be the Anchor Point Lighthouse was now going to be The Shipwreck Café, in honor of the ships that had been lost off Anchor Point in foul weather. Over a hundred ships had been smashed on the rocks and as many lives lost when the ships went down. The lighthouse had been decommissioned in 1999 and then privately bought where the property sat unused for fourteen years. Luckily for him, regular maintenance had been done on the buildings.

The ex-lighthouse keeper who owned it had died without fulfilling his dream of renovating the place into a bed and breakfast and museum. The estate put the place up for sale, where it finally came down to just two buyers; Jay, who wanted to preserve the place and turn it into a café, and a real estate company who wanted to tear it down and build condos in its place. The executor chose Jay even though his bid was lower. He knew his Dad, who had passed away, would want to preserve the tradition of the historical landmark.

Stormy, who had been sleeping contently next to Jay, lifted her head and snarled a low, throaty growl. Her head turned slowly like she was following something or someone moving through the cottage. Jay and Anna sat there, in stunned silence.

"I guess it's true," Anna whispered.

"Interesting," Jay exclaimed, watching the dog lay back down and close her eyes. "Whatever or whoever it was, is gone."

"Doesn't that freak you out?" asked Anna.

"No. As long as it doesn't bother me, I won't bother it," he answered, getting up off the floor. "Now, let's see if we can persuade Stormy to get into the car."

Jay removed a blanket from the trunk and spread it out on the front seat of the car. Stormy followed him out of the cottage and jumped into the car when requested. She turned in a circle several times, and then curled up into a ball on the seat.

"That wasn't too difficult," Anna added, smiling. "I think she knows she has a new friend."

"Let's see how much of a friend she thinks I am when we get to the vets," he declared, laughing. "I'll talk to you tomorrow."

He drove to the vet clinic on the edge of town. Leaving Stormy in the car, he went in to see if there were any open appointments for that day. When Jay explained that she had been abandoned and he was taking her in, the vet agreed to see Stormy in twenty minutes.

He climbed back into the car, and Stormy crawled over the shift and laid her head in his lap. She looked up at him with such sorrow in her eyes, Jay wished he could tell her that she was with him now and everything would be all right. He wanted to tell her that she would never be hungry or cold again, but he couldn't. All he could do was prove it over time.

Stormy limped painfully into her appointment, and they

discovered she weighed only thirty-two pounds. She was about twenty pounds underweight for her size and estimated age. The vet used a special machine to see if she was chipped and discovered she wasn't.

Sitting next to Jeremy in the small exam room, Stormy waited patiently for the doctor's visit. Doctor Carsen, a young woman in her late twenties, stepped through the door. She had long brown hair pulled back in a ponytail and was so petite in size that the white lab coat she wore engulfed her and hung down below her knees. She had a beautiful face with hazel eyes that mirrored the love and care she had for her animal patients. Kneeling next to the dog, she spoke softly while examining her.

"It looks like she stepped on a shell and sliced her paw. It's a long clean cut, probably from a razor clam shell. The cut needs to be cleaned out and wrapped. To be on the safe side, she should receive a series of shots to bring her up to date on her vaccines since we don't know if she has had any shots at all."

"What about her fur and the fleas? I am assuming that they are sand fleas," asked Jay, patting his new charge to keep her calm.

"She needs to be groomed; a full bath and flea dip would be the best thing for her. We can cut off the matted fur and brush her out. Our groomer will be in tomorrow; you could leave her here overnight and pick her up tomorrow at three," suggested the doctor.

"I would rather bring her home with me tonight. I don't want Stormy to think I'm deserting her, too. Would it be all right if I brought her back in the morning?"

"Sure. We can give the dog her shots right now. If you bring her back at ten in the morning, the groomer can give her the full spa treatment! Let's see if she'll let me look at that paw," the vet suggested.

Jay told Stormy to lay down, and she collapsed on to the floor.

"She must have had some kind of training," stated the vet. "I just don't understand humans. How could someone abandon such a beautiful dog?"

Jay continued to pat the dog and talk to her while her paw was being examined. Stormy never moved; it was almost as if she knew somehow that they were helping her. Dr. Carsen cleaned out the wound and spread some medicated salve on the paw before she wrapped it in gauze. Shots were administered as the dog calmly cooperated.

"Such a good girl," the vet approved, giving Stormy a treat. "We'll put a new dressing on the paw tomorrow after her bath. Try to keep her inside tonight and off the leg as much as possible."

"I'm going to take her to my cottage and keep her quiet for the night." answered Jay. "Thanks again, we'll see you tomorrow."

Jay picked out a pink collar from the rack and put it on Stormy. He decided to buy a matching leash, and placed it on the counter. He picked up a bag of dry dog food and a couple of cans of wet food as well. Some chew toys, balls, and tug of war toys rounded out the pile on the counter.

"This is going to be one spoiled dog," observed the receptionist, looking at the collection accumulating on the counter. "But, where's the treats?"

Jay added two different containers of treats to the mound, just to be on the safe side.

"I think that should do it for today," he said with a grin, taking out his credit card.

He guided Stormy back to the car. On the second trip, he returned with her dog supplies and stowed them in the back seat. The dog reclined on the blanket, carefully watching every move her new owner made. When Jay sat down in the driver's seat, Stormy jumped over the console and gave him a big wet kiss on the cheek.

"I guess this means we're friends," he said, laughing and wiping off the side of his face. "Let's go home, girl."

They arrived back at Jay's temporary home without further incident. He put the leash on her so she wouldn't run away now that she seemed to be feeling better. Once they were safely inside, he spread an old quilt on the floor next to his bed for her. Stormy laid down on her new bed and watched while he brought all her new things into the cottage.

Jay placed several treats and toys on the quilt with the dog. Stormy seemed to favor the stuffed toy duck; she tucked it under her chin and closed her eyes. The vet had said she would probably be lethargic from the shots. The contented dog let out a loud sigh and drifted off to sleep.

Her new owner stared at the sleeping dog and wondered how anyone could abuse and abandon such a wonderful animal. He would have to keep her on the leash for a while when they moved to the caretaker's cottage; at least until she understood that it was her forever home. He didn't want her to have a chance to run away. After a while, they could run the beach together and she could come and go as she pleased.

Grabbing a beer out of the refrigerator, Jeremy set to work on his business plans. His new life was taking shape. A new café, a new residence, and now a new companion to spend his time with. Things just couldn't get any better as far as Jeremy was concerned.

Chapter 2

FOR THE NEXT two weeks, Stormy, adorned with her pink collar and leash, accompanied Jay everywhere he went. Her coat was fluffy and full after her bath and groom. The sparkle had returned to her eyes and her tail wagged more often, and even her paw was healing up nicely. She still cringed occasionally when Jay reached to pat her, but that was happening less and less often. She had even started answering to the name "Stormy".

They spent every day at the cafe overseeing the renovation being done. Oftentimes while they walked around, Stormy would suddenly stop and growl, her head following something that apparently no one else could see. Her eyes always finally came to rest on the lighthouse door.

The lighthouse itself was short and wide, sixty-five feet tall from the base to the vent ball. The outside of the tower was built using limestone over a brick-lined interior. The exterior wall had been painted in red and white stripes in the early nineteen hundreds. There were no written records of exactly when it was painted, but it remained those colors to this day. There were small, staggered windows that ran to the top which allowed light to enter the interior structure to make climbing up the stairs safer.

Inside, a spiral staircase made up of seventy-six metal stairs wound up to the lantern room, which was then divided into three sections. The service room that housed the clockworks for the rotating beam, the vents, and in the old days the fuel tanks, was now an empty space. Large windows surrounded the service area allowing the keepers to watch out over the ocean while they worked.

Above this area was the heart of the lighthouse, the optic section. Glass windows called storm panes held in place by metal frames surrounded and protected the lens. A catwalk circumnavigated the optic section so the keepers could wash the exterior of the storm panes.

The third section was the dome. Clad in copper, it was the base for the vent ball which had a lightning rod perched on the top. Long ago, a wind vane sat on the top of the dome, but now only the base remained.

Most of the system was still intact, but hadn't been run since the decommissioning.

The romantic side of Jay came out when he decided to make the service area a private dining space with one table. Reservations for romantic wedding proposals would take precedent over all other requests. If no proposals were on the schedule, the table could be set up for four people to eat dinner and enjoy the experience.

The lighthouse was attached to a two-story building that Jay was turning into the café. The first floor was being split into two separate sections. A wall was being built to enclose a new state-of-the-art kitchen at the back of the building. The front section would house booths and tables for diners, and a small waiting area would be built to the right of the front door. People could enjoy a cocktail while they were waiting to be seated.

The second floor would be renovated into a bar and dining area. The wall overlooking the ocean would be ripped out and a continual panoramic window would be installed for people to look out while they dined. The bar was going to be built around the bones of an old tug boat that had been beached many years before on the point below.

New bathrooms would also be installed on both floors. An elevator for handicapped patrons would be installed near the bathrooms, and a second elevator would be put in adjacent to the kitchen for food delivery to the second floor.

Jay knew that a café was usually smaller in size than a restaurant, but he liked the sound of Shipwreck Café better than Shipwreck Restaurant. The name rolled off the tongue easier and was much catchier.

There were four other buildings on the property; Jay was going to use the keeper's cottage for his own personal residence. Another building just off the side of the café would eventually be turned into a gift shop that would sell the typical Cape Cod items that tourists looked for to take home as souvenirs.

A small winterized building would be utilized as a storage area and garage. Jay's truck would be fitted with a plow for winter months and stored in the garage during the summer.

Jay was saving the fourth building for Robbie. It was a smaller version of Jay's cottage. He was going to offer his younger brother a job and if he accepted, the cottage rent would be included in his pay. It would be the first year-round job that his brother would have ever held. Jay didn't know if Robbie was grown up enough to accept the offer. Since he was the baby of the family, he used the position to his advantage every chance he got.

Robert Hallett was a surfer. He had quit college after just two years and moved into his mother's basement. He worked part-time jobs when he felt like it and their mother supported him the rest of the time. It didn't seem to bother him that he was twenty-five years old and his mother was still cooking for him and doing his laundry. He was lazy and had made no effort to better his life.

By accepting this job, he could move out of their mother's basement and stop sponging off her. He could live in his own place, pay his own way, and give their Mom the break she deserved after raising them by herself since their father's death. She shouldn't still be babysitting a twenty-five-year-old.

Jay took out his cell and hit the button that would dial his brother's number.

"Hello."

"Robbie, what's up? Where are you?" asked his older brother.

"I'm playing video games. Why?"

"Can you meet me down at the point? I have something I need to talk to you about."

"Is something wrong? Is Mom okay?"

"Mom's fine. I have a new friend that I want you to come check out," Jay answered.

"I'll be there in ten minutes. I'll meet you at the picnic area."

"See you then. Don't screw around and not show up," warned Jay.

"Chill, I'll be there," Robbie replied.

Jay put Stormy on her leash and they set off for the picnic area located down below the lighthouse. He now owned all the land the picnic area sat on and a good-sized section of the beach that ran adjacent to it. The parking lot for both areas was also part of the parcel he purchased. It didn't seem right to Jay that the town could charge a fat fee for people to park on his land, to use his picnic area, and his beach. Over the past fourteen years, the town had collected fees for people to use the privately-owned land. He was going to have to figure out some way to beat the town at their own game and make the land available to everyone.

He sat on one of the tables and waited for his brother to arrive. He was late as usual. Stormy wanted to run so Jay let her leash lead out as far as it would go. Since she had to avoid the water until her foot healed, he made sure she stayed on dry land. Besides, it was only April, and the ocean hadn't heated up enough for swimming.

A car engine sputtered, signaling the approach of his brother. The bright yellow Jeep Robbie had bought right out of high school drove up the hill towards the meeting area. Jay couldn't believe the old Jeep was still running; it was ten years old when his brother had bought it used eight years ago. Then again, his brother never traveled any long distances. In fact, he never left town. The Jeep pulled up alongside the table and his brother jumped out.

Robert Hallett was your typical surfer dude. He had long blond hair, a body that would make any girl take a second look, and his skin was a golden bronze year-round. He had no ambitions in life except to hit the water and surf. He was twenty-five, but had the attitude and work ethic of a sixteen-year-old.

"What's up, Bro?" he asked, stretching out on the table. "Are you here on vacation?"

"No, I'm not. I live here now. I quit the firm and moved back to Anchor Point," Jay answered. "I've been here almost a month already."

"Seriously? Where have you been living? Why didn't you come back to Mom's?"

"I bought my own place."

Stormy came running up from the water's edge to the picnic table to check out the new human. She sniffed Robbie's feet that were hanging over the end of the table and backed away.

"Pretty bad, huh, Stormy?" Jay questioned, patting the dog's head as she sat down next to him.

"Is this your friend?" asked Robbie, sitting up.

"This is Stormy. Someone abandoned her and she's been living up at the lighthouse. Now, she lives with me," answered Jay. "She was abused. Don't make any fast moves near her or she'll think she's going to be hit."

"Poor thing. How did you find her? Was she down on the beach?" asked Robbie.

"No, she was sleeping on the back porch of the caretaker's cottage," he replied, smiling at the dog.

"Trespassing again, like when we were little?"

"No. I own the place now," he answered, looking for a reaction from his younger brother.

"Excuse me? You own the place? What does that mean exactly?" Robbie questioned.

"Precisely what I said. I own the lighthouse, all the surrounding buildings, and this picnic area and beach. It's all mine."

"Seriously, dude? You're joking, right?"

"I'm not joking. You are looking at the location of the new Shipwreck Café. I'm living in the old keeper's quarters. The lighthouse and its adjoining building are under renovations as we speak. And, I have an interesting offer to make you."

"An offer, dude? I'm still taking in the fact that you own this place," said Robbie shaking his head.

"I'm not dude. I'm Jay if you don't mind," his older brother responded curtly.

"Sorry, dude…I mean Jay," said Robbie.

When the brothers were little, Robbie couldn't say Jeremy. So, he started calling his brother Jay, and the name had stuck. Pretty much everyone in school had called him Jay. The attorney side of Jay wanted people to use his proper name, but he knew that being back on Anchor Point meant he'd have to get used to being hailed as Jay again.

Personally, Jay knew he had to work on letting the stiff attorney side of himself go. He was going to be a beachside restaurant owner now. The days of standing in a court of law in front of a judge were gone forever. He had better to learn to relax.

"What's this offer?" Robbie asked in consternation.

"Are you working right now?"

"Nope, vegging until the summer season starts," Robbie answered with a grin.

"Are you still in Mom's basement?"

"Yea, I am. Where's this going?" asked Robbie, sounding a

little defensive.

"I want to offer you a full-time job and a place of your own to live. There is another cottage behind mine that you could live in and it would be considered part of your pay package if you work here at the café."

"What would I be doing?" asked Robbie.

"I know you like to surf and spend your days on the beach during the summer. I was thinking you could be one of my bartenders five nights a week. It would be a full-time, year-round job. Your hours would be five P.M. to one A.M. each night."

"I don't know, Jay. I'm usually in bed by ten during the summer so I can hit the beach early," Robbie replied, looking out over the water.

"Where are you working this summer?"

"I don't know yet. I usually pick up a part-time job once everything opens."

"In other words, you'll work just enough to pay for your summer fun and then sponge off Mom again this coming winter," said Jay, getting angry. "When are you ever going to grow up?"

"I knew it was coming to this again," said Robbie angrily. "I haven't seen you for over a year and we are right back to where we left off."

"Robbie, you're twenty-five years old. You need a full-time job to support yourself. You're surfing lifestyle needs to be worked in around a job. If you were a professional surfer it would be different, but you're not. I'm offering you your own place to live, on the beach, and a year-round job at night so you can do what you want during the day."

"I'm going to have to think about it. What would my pay be?"

"Sixteen an hour plus tips. I know you worked as a bartender before and that you know what you are doing behind a bar. The other guy I hired at fourteen plus tips. You don't need to tell him you're making more than him if you decide to take the job. Plus, the cottage would be part of your package. It's a winterized cottage with a full kitchen."

"Can I look at the cottage I would be living in?" asked Robbie.

"Sure. Stormy and I will walk up and meet you there. Park in front of the lighthouse," Jay directed. "Come on, girl."

As Stormy led the way up the hill, Jay looked back and saw his brother was sitting in his Jeep staring at the ocean. Robbie answered his cell phone and did not look happy at what he was hearing. Jay heard the Jeep start up, but instead of coming up the hill, his brother drove the other way towards town.

"I guess he doesn't want the job," Jay confided to Stormy who looked at her owner, cocking her head. "Let's go home."

Living in the caretaker's cottage suited Jay. The walls were adorned with wooden planks from ships that had wrecked off the point over the years. The floors were old barn lumber. He had them sanded and refinished before he and Stormy had moved in. A fieldstone fireplace with a whale's jaw mantel was the centerpiece of the main living area. Jay had installed a small bar in the corner next to the fireplace for when he entertained.

A brown leather couch with a matching loveseat faced the fireplace. A ship's wheel end-table, with a recliner on each side sat in front of the windows that overlooked the beach behind the cottage. Stormy had her own large dog bed in front of the warm fireplace. A small den and half bath was to the right of the front door.

The kitchen was a good size, but outdated. Over time, Jay decided he would install new appliances and cabinets. A tigerwood trestle table had been left by the previous owners. A captain's chair, four other matching chairs, and a bench accompanied the table. The set looked like it was made specifically for the measurements of the room, although the age of the set was unknown or who it had originally belonged to. Jay loved the old-fashioned feel that the table set gave to the kitchen and decided to keep it.

There were two bedrooms on the second floor, one of which Jay was currently using as an office. Stormy had a dog bed in each of the rooms. She never used the one in Jay's bedroom; every night she beat her master onto the bed and he never had the heart to make her get down.

He left Stormy eating her supper and went to lock up the café building. He arrived as the last worker was leaving.

"Man, there's some weird things going on in this place," the electrician confessed.

"What do you mean?" asked Jay.

"A couple of times today I set a tool down and came back minutes later to get it and it had disappeared," he explained. "I still haven't found my wire cutters."

"Did someone else use them and not tell you?" asked Jay, not wanting to let on that he thought the place was haunted.

"I don't think so. What's even crazier is I thought I saw a guy in a black suit standing at the door to the lighthouse. The suit had long tails and looked like it was from another era. He was watching everything I was doing. When I walked over to see who he was, he was gone."

"Did anything else happen?" asked Jay.

"No, not to me. But, when two of my guys were checking the service area up in the lighthouse, they thought they heard a man's voice asking them what they were doing. If I didn't know better, I would say this place is haunted," he said, chuckling.

"You just never know, do you?" Jay asked, smiling.

"No, you don't. We'll see you tomorrow. Have a good night," he added, heading out the café door.

Jay walked around observing what work had been performed. It was coming along nicely and looked to be on schedule for completion. He walked through the swinging doors to the new kitchen; the space was beginning to look like a real working kitchen. Appliances had been delivered and were in place. Long metal counters had been built around the perimeter of the kitchen for storage. The new pizza oven was sitting in the middle of the room not yet hooked up.

He turned to leave the area and heard his name being called. A man's voice, loud and clear, spoke his name a second time. His heart raced; he didn't want to turn around in case the man in the black suit was standing there. He wasn't ready to face the ghost just yet, not until he knew more about him. As calmly as he could, he walked out of the kitchen, out the front door of the café, and took the path to his cottage.

Stormy met him at the door, tail wagging. Jay walked over to the fridge, reached in, and grabbed a beer. He plopped on the couch and opened the twist-off cap. The dog laid her chin on his leg, watching him with soulful eyes.

"I can't let this get to me," he said to Stormy. "I have to face him sooner or later."

Jay sat there drinking his beer and trying to relax. He started to calm down and think about something else when a loud knocking sounded on the front door. He just about jumped out of his skin as Stormy ran to the door barking.

Chapter 3

JAY JUMPED OFF the couch. He wrenched the front door open and was face to face with one pissed-off brother.

"You knew this was happening, didn't you?" yelled Robbie, pushing his way through the door.

Stormy didn't like the loud voice and ran quickly to hide behind the couch. Jay followed her to make sure she was all right, but she was quivering all over. He tried to pat her and calm her down, but she shied away from his touch. Jay figured the past owners must have yelled at her when they abused her. He stood up, glaring at his younger brother.

"What the hell is wrong with you? I told you she was abused and you come in here yelling like a madman," said Jay in a monotone voice so as not to scare the dog any more than she already was.

"I'm sorry. I forgot about Stormy being here. I didn't mean to scare her."

"Well, you did. Two weeks of working with her is out the window, thanks to you," Jay scolded, sitting on the floor next to Stormy. "It's okay, girl. No one is going to hurt you."

Robbie walked around the end of the couch and sat on the floor next to his brother. The dog lifted her head and eyed him suspiciously. He reached his hand out very slowly.

"I'm really sorry, Jay. I would never do anything to hurt Stormy. I was just mad."

"Mad about what? What do I supposedly know is happening?"

"Mom. She's leaving the Cape," Robbie replied angrily.

"What do you mean she's leaving?"

Stormy had calmed down enough to lay beside Jay's leg. She closed her eyes in ecstasy as Jay gently patted her.

"You really don't know, do you?" asked Robbie in a confused voice.

"I don't have any idea what you are talking about."

"Mom put the house up for sale three months ago, but didn't tell me. Apparently, she got an offer on the house for the full amount. She's moving to Florida with her best friend, Theresa."

"Seriously? She didn't even tell you she put it up for sale? That was harsh."

"Yea, you think? The closing is May fifteenth. I have to be out of the basement by May tenth. I was mad because I thought you and Mom had ganged up on me and planned this whole setup about the cottage and the job."

"Mom doesn't even know I bought this place. I was going to finish it and bring her up here on opening night. Now, she won't even be here for it. Man, that so sucks."

"She knows you're back. Where does she think you are living?"

"She thinks I'm staying at Grampa's old cottage on Run Hill Road."

"Are you going to tell her now that she's leaving?"

"I'll bring her up here tomorrow and show her the place," said Jay. "Does that mean you are taking me up on my offer?"

"I'm going to have to. I can't find anywhere else to live on such short notice. All the J-1s are arriving and places are filling up quickly. Trying to find a place to live on Cape Cod this close to summer is damn near impossible."

"Come on over tomorrow and I'll show you the cottage."

A loud scraping noise came from the kitchen. Stormy stood up, stared in the direction of the kitchen, and growled low in her throat.

"What was that?" asked Robbie, looking at the dog.

The brothers walked to the kitchen door and Jay looked around to see if anything was out of place. The captain's chair at the head of the table had been pulled out as if someone was sitting in it, waiting for supper to be served. Stormy was still growling in the living room.

"This is my house now," Jay stated firmly. "You are more than welcome to stay in the lighthouse. Stormy and I live here, not you."

"Ah, Jay, who are you talking to?" asked his younger brother.

"I'm not sure yet," he answered. "I have to check out the history of this place. All I know is that the place is supposedly haunted by a man in a black suit."

"Haunted?"

The chair moved again, like someone was pushing back on it to get up and leave the table. The brothers watched the back door to the cottage open and close by itself. Stormy stopped growling and walked into the kitchen.

"Tell me I didn't just see that happen," Robbie said shakily.

"Kind of cool, ha?" asked Jay. "I was going to cook some supper. Want to grab a steak with me and Stormy?"

"Jay, doesn't that bother you? I don't know if I can live here or not," Robbie muttered, shaking his head.

"He isn't going to hurt you. He thinks he still lives here. Besides, I don't think he'll come to your cottage. It wasn't built when he was the lighthouse keeper."

"I can't understand how you're so calm about this. I never believed in ghosts until just now. If I hadn't seen it with my own eyes..." said Robbie. "Can I have a beer?"

"It's in the fridge. Help yourself. Are you staying for supper or not?" Jay queried.

Jay pushed the captain's chair back under the table where it belonged. He started cooking the steaks and throwing together a tossed salad. Robbie sat down in one of the side chairs at the table, not wanting to sit in the chair that had moved all by itself. Stormy laid at Jay's feet, waiting for something yummy to drop that she could claim as her own.

"Have you seen this ghost yet?" Robbie questioned.

"I haven't, but the electrician did over in the café. The keeper tried to talk to me in the kitchen."

"He talked to you?"

"Kind of. He called out my name twice. I wasn't ready to confront him yet, so I left the café and came back here. A lot of good that did. Apparently, he comes in here, too," said Jay, setting the salad on the table. "I was trying to set boundaries tonight by telling him that this was my house now. Time will tell if it worked."

"Do you think he'll come back tonight?" asked Robbie, looking around.

"Don't worry about it. Have another beer. The steaks are just about done."

The two brothers had a great time visiting during supper. It had been a long time since they had spent any time together without fighting and arguing. Stormy laid under the table quietly. Robbie made a new friend slipping her pieces of steak when Jay wasn't looking.

It was decided that Robbie would move into the cottage at the beginning of May. He would start to work at the same time, helping to set up the bar area and order what liquor was needed for opening night. He had been a bartender before and knew what it would take to run a full bar. It was the first time Jay had ever seen his younger brother excited about a job. Maybe it was because Jay gave him the title of Bar Manager.

The grand opening was scheduled for Saturday, June first, which was only six weeks away. Staff had to be hired and trained, supplies ordered, and finishing touches completed. Robbie could help to accomplish a lot of the remaining work.

Jay promised him a future partnership if things panned out.

Before Robbie left, they agreed to meet at the lighthouse at ten the next morning. Jay would pick up their Mom and bring her up for the grand tour and Robbie would get his first tour at the same time. He promised his older brother he wouldn't say a word when he went home about the big reveal.

Stormy jumped up on the bed and was waiting for Jay as he came out of the bathroom, turned off the lights, and crawled into bed. They slept through the night thankfully undisturbed.

The next morning, Jay pulled up to twelve Sea Call Way to pick up his Mom. Martha Hallett was fifty-seven years old. She was a pretty woman whose face showed her life's story of working two and three jobs to bring up her boys and put them through school. Martha was an avid tennis player and in great shape. She worked at To Dye For, the local beauty shop as its receptionist. She and her best friend Theresa could be found playing bingo three nights a week. She loved her two boys and had always wanted nothing but the best for them.

Jay insisted on blindfolding his mother for the big surprise. Being the good sport that she was, she went along with it and crawled into the car.

"This is crazy," said his Mom as they drove. "You move home as I am leaving for Florida. At least I know that you and your brother have each other and are finally on better speaking terms."

"He's going to meet us there," Jay informed her, careful not to give anything away.

"Thank you for giving him a job and a place to live. I was worried about leaving him. Robbie hasn't grown up like you have. I had visions of him sleeping on the beach this winter, but I had to do something to force his hand. Just don't tell him I said that."

"He's going to be fine. You don't have to worry about him," said Jay.

"What I can't figure out, is what kind of job you gave him?" his Mom asked.

"You'll see; we are almost there. Two more minutes."

Jay turned up the long dirt road that led to the lighthouse. He could see Robbie's Jeep parked in front of the building.

"He's actually on time," mumbled Jay in surprise.

"Are you talking to me?" asked his Mom.

"No, I'm not. We're here. Keep the blindfold on until I get you out of the car, okay?"

"This must be some surprise," his Mom replied, chuckling.

The mother and two sons stood side by side in the sunlight.

"This is something I have wanted for a long time, Mom. Robbie's going to be part of the adventure, which makes me extremely happy. I just wish you were going to be around to see it happen."

With a flourish, Jay removed his Mom's blindfold. She blinked a few times as her eyes grew accustomed to the bright sunshine, and her mouth dropped open in surprise.

"I don't understand. You bought the Anchor Point Lighthouse?" she asked in astonishment.

"Yes, I did. You are looking at the new Shipwreck Café. I'm living in the keeper's cottage and Robbie will be living in the smaller cottage behind mine. Do you want a tour?" asked Jay, trying to read the expression on his mother's face.

"I would love a tour. I have lived here my whole life and never been inside the lighthouse. They say it's haunted. Have you run into any ghosts?" Mom queried.

"Have we ever!" Robbie answered with a shiver.

"You seriously have? You know your grandmother was a psychic. I didn't inherit her gift, but they say it skips a generation. Maybe, you two boys got her gift and have the ability to see and communicate with spirits."

"Man, that's one gift I'd rather pass on," Robbie replied.

"You have to put on a hard hat because there is a lot of

construction going on inside," Jay requested, passing out hats to both of them.

He took his mother's arm and led her inside the main building and Robbie followed behind. They toured the main dining area, the new kitchen, and the second floor where they were just installing the new windows. The bar area was complete. Robbie was impressed with the size of the bar and that is was built around the bones of the tugboat they used to play on as kids. He told his mother several times that his title was Bar Manager; she could see he was very proud of his new job.

"We can take you up into the lighthouse if you want, Mom," said Jay. "But, it's seventy-six steps up to the top. Can you make it okay?"

"You bet I can. It may be the only time I ever get a chance to go to the top of a lighthouse. Lead the way."

They started up the metal stairs as their footsteps echoed in the shell of the structure. They stopped halfway up so their mother could rest. The only problem was, they had stopped, but the footsteps didn't. Robbie looked like he was going to lose it, but his Mom patted his arm to calm him down. They stood still listening as the footsteps got closer and closer to where they were standing. A cold air swirled by them, but there were no windows close enough to explain the sudden cold breeze. The footsteps continued for another twenty seconds, and then stopped abruptly.

"Robbie, you okay to keep going? Mom, how about you?" asked Jay.

"I'm good," Mom answered shakily. "I do believe I just met a ghost. Theresa will never believe me. You know, Jay, this would be a great draw for the café; people love haunted places."

As they reached the service room, Robbie stayed close to Jay. Martha wandered around looking out the arched windows to the ocean vista below.

"Mom, don't get too close to the windows. The crew hasn't

been up here yet to install the safety bars," warned Jay.

"It's so beautiful. You can see the whole point from up here. It must be gorgeous at night," Mom observed. "I still think it would be a great calling card to say the place was haunted. People would come from all over for a chance to see a ghost."

"I have to research the history of the place first. I don't even know the name of the keeper in the black suit who haunts this place," Jay responded.

As if off in the far distance, a voice distinctly said, "Roland."

"I think you just got your answer," Martha observed with a shiver.

"I need to leave, like now," said Robbie, heading for the stairs. "Maybe you think this is cool, but I'm a little freaked out right now."

"We'll all head down. Ready, Mom?" asked Jay. "Lead the way, Robbie."

Back on the ground, the group went to see Jay's new residence. Martha met Stormy and instantly fell in love with her. The dog accompanied them to Robbie's new place; a much smaller version of Jay's home, but still ten times bigger than the basement he had been living in. He couldn't wait to move in, ghost or no ghost.

"Where's Stormy?" asked Jay.

"I think I saw her head out the back door," Martha answered.

Jay walked to the door and stopped just inside. He stood watching Stormy who looked like she was playing with someone. Her butt end was sticking up in the air, tail wagging, and her front paws were stretched out in front of her like she was waiting for a ball to be thrown. She pranced around in a circle, sat as if on command, and then pranced some more. Martha had been watching the dog through the window. She put her fingers over her lips signaling to Jay to keep this little diversion to himself.

"Come on, girl. Want to go for a ride?" asked Jay.

Stormy looked at Jay. She glanced back to where she had been looking, but the ghost must have disappeared. The dog wandered into the house and plopped down next to Jay.

"I think we may have more than one ghost," whispered Jay. "Stormy doesn't like the lighthouse keeper and growls every time he is near. But she does seem to like whoever this new ghost is."

"You need to go speak to Bea Thomas at the historical society about this. She knows everything there is to know about this town and its history. If she doesn't know off the top of her head, she knows where to find the information," Martha advised.

"I love this place," said Robbie, stepping into the room. "I can see the beach from my bedroom window."

"It's kind of empty," Jay observed.

"It's okay. He can have most of the furniture from my house. I'm going to buy all new things when I get to Florida," Martha offered. "Robbie, can you take me home now?"

"Sure, Mom."

"Robbie, I am going to start interviewing people tomorrow. Can you be available to help me?" Jay requested.

"I told Paul I'd meet up with him for some surfing at nine. What time do you need me?"

"Eleven is good. I have fourteen applicants for the eight bartender positions. I figured you could talk to them and tell me who we should hire," he answered. "Even though you'll be on the schedule for some shifts, most of the time you'll be busy doing other things and not behind the bar."

"I'll be here," Robbie promised.

"It's nice to be able to leave for Florida knowing my sons are on better terms," Mom said, tearing up. "Your Dad would be so proud of you both right now."

"Exactly when are you leaving for Florida?" asked Jay.

"I was going to leave on the twentieth of May after the closing. But for now, I need to stick around to be here for the grand opening of The Shipwreck Café. I want to be the first one to order a drink from the new Bartender Manager," she answered with a huge grin.

"Do you want to stay upstairs in the spare room until you leave?" asked Jay.

"I'll let you know. I have to check with Theresa and see if she wants to stay or meet me down there."

"Okay. Love you," Jay replied, kissing her on the cheek.

"See you in the morning," offered Robbie as he headed out the door.

Jay and Stormy stood in the doorway together. It was strange watching his Mom climb up into the Jeep; he didn't realize how old she had gotten over the years that he was in Boston. She was still in good shape, but older. Jay would have to make it a point to spend as much time with his Mom as he could before she left for Florida. He was sad that now that he was back home she wouldn't be here.

"Come on, girl. Let's go for a ride to the historical society."

Chapter 4

THE ANCHOR POINT National Historical Society was housed in a small building on the edge of town. Once an old lobster shanty, it was weather beaten on the outside, but pristine on the inside. Rows of file cabinets and book shelves filled with a veritable wealth of information lined the walls. Maps encased in plastic for protection hung on racks next to the desk at the head of the room. Two tables with chairs stood in the center of the suite.

Jay walked in with Stormy on her leash. Bea Thomas, the town historian, was busy rifling through files and turned when the door closed loudly behind Jay. She eyed the dog warily.

"I hope it's okay I have Stormy with me; she's very well trained," he said, smiling that big old grin of his.

"I guess it's all right. There's no signs posted against dogs. No one has ever brought one in before. Just don't let her pee on the floor," said Bea. "Aren't you Jay Hallett? All grown up, aren't you?"

"Yes, ma'am, I am. My Mom told me if I needed help finding out information on the Anchor Point Lighthouse, I should come to you."

"Someone just bought that place. After all the years of it being abandoned, I heard it's being turned into a restaurant."

"Yes, that's true. I bought the place," the new owner smiled proudly. "The Shipwreck Café will open on June first."

"You bought the place? I thought you were some big-wig attorney up in Boston," she sniffed, peering over her glasses.

"No offense meant."

"None taken. I am, I mean I was. I quit the firm to move back here. The law and I just didn't agree on many occasions. I couldn't justify defending law breakers that could buy high-priced attorneys who would twist the laws to suit their needs," said Jay. "I'm running the restaurant now."

"An attorney with ethics? You are definitely better off running a restaurant," Bea commented, closing the file cabinet. "What do you need to know about the lighthouse?"

"It seems I have bought a property that appears to be haunted. Do you know anything about any ghosts hanging around the lighthouse?" asked Jay.

"Why, have you seen any?" Bea questioned skeptically.

"I haven't actually seen them, but I have been in the room when they have been there. Stormy is the one who can see them," he confided, patting the dog.

"They say animals are more sensitive to spirits than humans are," Bea stated, pulling out a large leather-bound album and setting it on the table.

"Stormy seems to like one of the spirits and not the other," Jay asserted as he walked towards the table.

"If my memory serves me right, I believe there are at least five ghosts up at the lighthouse and down on the beach under the point. Over the years, they have been seen in different places at different times. Here is your first supposed ghost," she indicated, pointing to a portrait in the book.

"Roland Knowles. He was the lighthouse keeper from eighteen-eighty-five to nineteen-ten," Jay read the caption under the picture.

"He probably would have been there until he died of natural causes if someone hadn't murdered him," said Bea, shaking her head.

"Murdered him? How was he murdered?" asked Jay.

"Someone pushed him over the catwalk on the lighthouse,"

she answered cryptically.

"How do you know he didn't just fall?"

"It was a dark and stormy night. Roland was up checking the panes, making sure everything was intact. He always tied a rope around himself to go out on the catwalk in windy weather. Someone pushed him off and as he was dangling, this person cut the rope and he fell to his death. They found him the next morning with the cut rope still tied around his waist."

"Did they ever found out who did it or why?" Jay wondered.

"No one was ever charged. Speculation was that it was done because he wouldn't tell whoever was holding the knife above him where he hid the treasure. I think I have another book with a story about the fortune he found out on the point," Bea offered, heading to the room marked with a "Private" sign above the door.

Jay looked at the full-length portrait. He was a distinguished looking man with dark hair. Piercing black eyes and a square chin gave him a menacing look. It was no wonder that Stormy had growled at him. He was wearing a black suit with tails just like the electrician had described.

Jay flipped the page to a closer shot that showed Roland from the waist up. Instead of a coat, he was wearing a black vest and a white dress shirt. He held a fancy pocket watch in his right hand that hung on a chain attached to his vest. A black cap was pulled down low on his forehead.

Bea came out of the back room carrying several books. She set them on the table and took a seat. Small in stature, grey hair drawn up in a bun, and seventy-five years old, she was out of breath from carrying the heavy annuals to the table.

"He was a scary looking man," Jay observed, chuckling.

"I think it was just the era. Back then, men were men. He took the responsibilities of his job very seriously. He never married. His life was the lighthouse and keeping ships away from the point," Bea continued. "It is said that he fell apart and publicly cried when The Fallen Mist crashed on the rocks and over forty lives were lost. After the storm broke he was the first one on the beach collecting the bodies that washed ashore. Many were women and children that had sailed here from Ireland."

"He still thinks he's on duty, ha, girl?" Jay asked, talking to the dog. "Are there any children's ghosts reported to haunt the place?"

"I think you are the only one that has ever asked me that. Recorded in the ship's manifest is a young girl named Colleen O'Mara who was ten years old when she was lost on the Mist. People have seen her running the beach, calling for her mother or up on the point looking out over the ocean. The place has been abandoned so long that the ghosts and the treasure have all but been forgotten about. Why do you ask?"

"Stormy growls whenever the keeper is around. This morning she was playing with someone on the upper point. We couldn't see who it was, but my mother and I watched the dog sitting on command, running in circles around someone, and wagging her tail like she knew them."

"You couldn't see them? Maybe, she was playing with herself," suggested Bea who was not one to believe in ghosts. "Animals have been known to amuse themselves when no one else is around."

"No, she was definitely listening to someone," stated Jay. "So, what about this treasure you mentioned?"

"Now, where are those newspaper clippings?" muttered Bea, flipping through one of the ledgers. "I know they are in this volume."

"You said Roland Knowles found it buried out on the point? Didn't the government still own the land at that time?" asked Jay, his curiosity piqued. "So why was he allowed to keep the treasure?"

"It's all in the story here," Bea disclosed, pointing to a clipping out of The Anchor Point Chronicles which had gone defunct back in nineteen-thirty-five. "I don't think it was ever found after Roland hid it. He didn't live a wealthy man's life, so it was assumed he never spent it."

"You mean I bought property that might be hiding a buried treasure?" he asked excitedly. "Ghosts and buried treasure, how cool is that?"

"Cool if you believe in those sorts of things," Bea sniffed again, adjusting her glasses and shaking her head. "Not too many people know about the treasure now-a-days. If you're smart, you will keep it that way, otherwise you will have people digging everywhere on your land looking for it."

"Good point," agreed Jay. "Do you mind if we stay here and read about it all for a while?"

"That's what we're here for," said the elderly woman, standing up. "I have filing to do. Make sure you sign your name in the guest book. We like to keep track of who visits. Call me if you need anything else."

Stormy laid under the table while Jay read, fascinated by the history. If there was any truth to the story, Knowles found the chest at low tide in a cave located under the point. He claimed it was below water level when found and that no one owns the ocean. There was no way to prove what ship the gold came from as many pirates were active in the area at the time. He fought the government and it was ruled they had no claim to the treasure; Roland Knowles was the rightful owner.

Gold coins and bars, loose gems, and gold jewelry inlaid with more gems were nestled in the chest he uncovered. Back in nineteen-o-nine its estimated worth was half a million dollars. There was only one known picture of the treasure and that had disappeared years ago.

"At today's gold prices, I would say that treasure is worth around thirty million, give or take," Jay revealed to the dog. "I wonder if it's still on the property somewhere?"

"I'm going to lunch," Bea stated, coming out of the back

room. "Are you almost done?"

"Just one more quick question?" Jay entreated, pushing back his chair.

"Do I believe the treasure is somewhere still around? I doubt it. It was probably found years ago, and no one said anything so they didn't get killed for it."

"Actually, I was going to ask you who the other ghosts were. You said there were five haunting the property."

"Mind you, I don't believe in ghosts myself. Never seen one, never care to. But, per the stories over the years, there are five ghosts. Roland Knowles and Colleen O'Mara are the first two. The other three were seen down on the lower point. The descriptions over the years have varied. Their outfits would date them from the mid to late eighteen-hundreds. Most people who have seen them say they look like pirates."

"Most of the lower point is under water now," Jay offered, thinking out loud.

"That's probably why they haven't been seen for years," stated Bea as her stomach growled loudly. "Anything else?"

"No, you have been a big help. Do you want help carrying those books to the back room before I go?"

"No, it will give me something to do when I get back from lunch. Say hi to your Mom for me. I haven't seen her at bingo lately," Bea responded, flipping the "Open" sign to "Closed".

"Mom's moving to Florida," Jay informed her on his way out the door.

"You don't say? You make sure you tell her to come say goodbye to me before she leaves," Bea insisted, locking the door. "Florida takes another local. Humph, we are becoming a vanishing breed around here."

"Yes, we are, Bea. Yes, we are," agreed Jay. "Make sure you come to the grand opening on June first. Your first drink is on me."

"I wouldn't miss it. I think the whole town will be there,"

Bea commented, walking away with a wave of her hand.

Stormy had been such a good dog while they were at the historical society, that Jay decided to reward her. It was dead low tide. He was going to take her to the lower point and let her run while he checked out the area that was usually under water. He parked next to the picnic area and opened the door to let her out. She took off running down the beach; Jay had to jog at a fast pace just to keep her in sight.

He rounded the point to see Stormy staring at the cliff up above. This time Jay saw her. A young girl with long braids in a calf length dress was standing there staring out over the water. She smiled at Stormy and then saw Jay standing there; she vanished in less than a second. A shiver went up Jay's spine; this was the very first time he had actually seen a ghost. He stood there staring, waiting for her to come back. The dog started to run again, signaling to Jay that the ghost was gone.

Stormy was bounding in and out of the water. She found a ball that had been left behind by someone else and claimed it as her own. As she played, Jay checked out the underside of the point, occasionally staring upwards to see if the ghost was watching him. He just couldn't shake the feeling there were eyes following him. He went back to exploring to keep his mind occupied.

The pounding tides changed the surface of the lower point every day. The under cliffs were comprised off soft clay, sand, and some rock. Every year, the point unfortunately lost another several feet to the ocean. Fierce winter storms were the worst; they accounted for a large amount of the footage lost.

Jay wondered how many more caves were concealed in the cliffs. The articles at the historical society stated that Knowles found the treasure chest in a small cave under the rocky overhangs. Any caves that were here a hundred years ago were already claimed by the ocean and its fury.

As much as this treasure hunt captured Jay's interest, he

knew he had a restaurant to get ready to open. Applications had to be printed off the computer and sorted into positions to be filled. Interviews started the following day and Jay wanted to look over the people who had applied to get a first impression. Robbie was going to help with the bar interviews, but Jay had to handle the rest.

Two executive chefs, eight sous chefs, three hostesses, and at least twenty waitresses had to be hired and trained as soon as possible. The café kitchen and dining rooms would be completed next week; that left two weeks for training before the grand opening on June first.

Jay had put together a selection of foods he wanted to serve at the café. Once he hired his two executive chefs, they would sit down and finalize the menu. Fresh seafood dinners would be the highlights of the café. Jay had already opened a store account with Cappy, the owner of the fish store on the docks, to purchase the fresh seafood daily right off the boats.

His mother's homemade clam chowder recipe would be on the menu every night. Made with bacon and other secret ingredients, it was loved by whoever ate it. Jay and one sous chef would have the recipe and be responsible for making the chowder fresh every morning. No one else would have access to the ingredients.

Various other steak, chicken, and Italian dinners would also be offered. A full appetizer menu along with an extensive dessert menu would complete the food listings. The fully loaded bar would accommodate any type of drink ordered. A wine locker had been installed in the cellar of the building. Jay wanted The Shipwreck Café to be known far and wide as a five-star dining restaurant.

"Come on, Stormy. It's time to go home," yelled Jay.

The dog picked up the ball and trotted over to her owner.

"I'll race you back to the car, girl. Bye, Colleen" Jay hollered, waving towards the upper cliff and taking off in a run.

The crews were busy at work in the café and the lighthouse. After checking in with the foreman, Jay retired to the office in his cottage to start working on the applications. Stormy curled up on her bed next to the desk, exhausted from her play time on the beach. The computer printer ran steadily for the next two hours. He sent out emails setting a specific time for each applicant to show up for an interview. Four hours later he had finally set up all the interviews that would span over the next five days. It was time to call it a night and lock up the café building.

It was dark and all the workers had quit for the night. Jay didn't want to go in by himself, not just yet. He knew he would have to get over his fear of Roland. There would be many nights he would have to close the café by himself. He just needed a little more time. But unfortunately, Roland had other ideas.

Chapter 5

JAY PULLED ON the door to make sure it was closed tightly. As he turned the key to lock the door, there was a loud crash from inside the café. He stood there, trying to muster up the courage to go inside and see what had caused the noise. He opened the door, reached his hand in to flip on the lights, and stood just inside the doorway, looking around.

A tall aluminum ladder lay on its side in the middle of the room. Behind the fallen ladder stood the ghost of Roland Knowles. They stared at each other for several seconds; Jay figured it was now or never to confront his fear.

"What do you want, Roland?" asked Jay, trying not to let his voice quiver.

"I want quiet."

Jay could hear the words being spoken, but didn't see Roland's lips moving. He decided to tell the ghost exactly how it was going to be in the future. It was better to see his reaction now rather than in front of paying customers.

"Mr. Knowles, I understand that you have lived here in peaceful solitude for the last fifteen years. That is going to change. I own this property now, and I am opening a restaurant. There will be many people hustling in and out and a lot of noise."

The ghost continued to stare at Jay.

"You are welcome to stay here. However, I don't want you to cause harm to any of my customers or staff, nor do I want you to destroy any of my property. Do you understand?"

Roland floated over to the door connecting the café to the lighthouse. Jay could hear the footsteps begin and end as Roland moved across the room. The ghost turned.

"I want quiet," he repeated as he passed through the wooden door that led to his beloved lighthouse.

Knowing that the ghost was gone, Jay stood the ladder back up. He looked around to see if anything else had been disturbed. Seeing nothing else out of place, he shut off the lights, and locked the door. He returned to his cottage and grabbed a beer from the fridge. Stormy jumped up on the couch and cuddled close to him.

"I did it, girl," he said, stroking the dog. "I faced Roland Knowles and didn't run. I don't think he was too happy with what I said to him, though. We'll have to wait and see his reaction."

Jay sat there drinking his beer feeling pretty proud of himself. He closed his eyes and relaxed. When Stormy sat up and started to growl, Jay knew that Roland couldn't be far away. He heard footsteps upstairs and loud noises emanating from his office. He dashed up the stairs two at a time.

He opened the door, which he didn't remember closing, and ran into the room. The neat stacks of applications had been blown everywhere. Everything that had been on his desk was on the floor. Stormy stood in the doorway, hair on end, growling fiercely. A book came flying off the shelf aimed at Jay's head. That did it- now Jay was really mad.

"Roland, I told you this was my home now. You have no right to come in here and destroy my things. I know you are still here and can hear me. Things have changed. I said you were welcome to stay here, but on my terms only. Go back to the lighthouse; you don't belong in this cottage anymore. Stay out! Do you hear me?"

Everything went quiet. Stormy stopped her growling and sat down. Jay looked around in despair; it would take him all night to put things back in place. Luckily, he had stapled the pages of the individual applications together. It would just be a matter of sorting them back into the piles of jobs applied for.

He moved things around on the floor looking for one specific item that was missing. When he found it, tears welled up in his eyes. Sitting on the floor, he held the two pieces in his hands and cried like a baby.

One of the few things he had of his Dad's was his favorite pipe. Growing up, Jay could remember his Dad coming home after work, eating supper, and then reading the paper while smoking his pipe. The sweet smell of Captain Black tobacco would fill the house. The pipe, cradled carefully in a wooden holder, had been displayed on Jay's desk.

The worshipped memory of his Dad was now broken into two pieces. The wooden holder had been slammed against the wall and broken as well. The more Jay cried, the more he despised the ghost. Suddenly, Stormy started to growl again.

Jay looked up. The ghost was standing in the corner of the room watching him. Filled with rage, Jay stood up with his Dad's pipe in his hand.

"See this? This was my Dad's. It was one of the few things I had left that reminded me of him. And now, in your childlike fit of anger, you have destroyed it. I don't even think I can fix it, the wood is so shattered. Get out of my house and don't you come back, ever," Jay yelled, falling back to the floor clutching the pieces of pipe to his chest.

The ghost floated over to where he was sitting on the floor. Jay looked up at him with tears rolling down his cheeks. Roland stared at the young man with true sorrow in his eyes.

"I'm sorry," he whispered as he vanished.

Three hours later Jay had the office cleaned up and the applications sorted for the next day's interviews. He fell into bed at two in the morning.

Six o'clock came early. Jay showered, ate breakfast, fed the dog, and went upstairs to get the applications. The first ones to be interviewed were the people for the executive chef's positions. He walked to the desk to grab the pile of corresponding paperwork.

Sitting in the center of the blotter was a pipe. It looked like an antique; the stem was carved out of what appeared to be whale bone. The wooden bowl had a whaling ship carved into one side with a date of nineteen-hundred carved on the opposite side. Jay was certain he had never seen it before. Then it hit him; it was a peace offering from the ghost.

The pipe must have belonged to Roland when he lived here. It must have been hidden away all these years, probably in the lighthouse, and now, he was offering it to Jay as a gift. It was handmade and obviously well taken care of.

"Roland, the pipe is beautiful. Thank you. I hope this means we can live together in peace. It will be busy and noisy for a good portion of the day and night. But, late at night it will be quiet with no one around to bother you. I hope we can work this out," Jay offered up as he set the old pipe next to his Dad's broken pipe.

He turned to leave and had that feeling of eyes watching him again. He looked around the room, but couldn't see anyone. Roland was in the room; Jay could sense him. Then, in a snap, he was gone.

Stormy followed Jay to the café and they settled into the hostess area waiting for the first applicant. It wasn't long before he walked through the door. Jay stood up and extended his hand.

"Tyrone Fenster, nice to meet you," he said shaking Jay's hand. "People call me Ty."

"Ty, you have an extensive resume. Why did you leave your last job at The Carriage House?" Jay inquired, sitting down.

"I wanted to leave Philadelphia. It's not like it used to be; I lived in a rough neighborhood where I was robbed at knife point twice in the last year. I decided I had had enough," he answered.

"My family is originally from the Cape, but I haven't been back here since I was six."

"It's changed a lot here. Not many locals left, mostly wash-a-shores now. And housing prices are out of control. Do you have somewhere to live if you're hired?" Jay asked with interest.

"I rented a house up on the beach about a mile up the road. I figured I would stay for at least the summer even if I didn't get the year-round job at this place," he answered. "I have two extra bedrooms and a finished cellar for another two or three cots if someone else needs somewhere to live. It would sure be nice to have help with the rent."

"What is your signature dish?"

"I love all seafood, but scallops are my specialty. I make a broiled scallop in white wine, garlic sauce that's to die for. My herb crab stuffing was voted number one in The Philadelphia Food Guide three years running."

"How long have you held the position of executive chef?"

"Fourteen years. I know my way around a kitchen and how to deal with kitchen staff," Ty answered.

"Here's the tentative menu," Jay offered, sliding it to Ty. "What do you think? Truthfully?"

"It's a good start. It needs to be tightened up. That's a big appetizer menu. I take it there is a bar in this place, thus the need for so many appetizers."

"There is a bar on the second floor. Do you think there's too many?"

"In my experience, it's better to start out small and add to the menu by offering nightly specials. If they sell well, you can make them a permanent item on the menu. Offer vegetables that are in season because they are cheaper."

"Sounds like good advice. Do you want to see the kitchen? It's not quite done yet, but you can get the feel of it," Jay suggested.

"That would be great," Ty agreed.

The two men strolled into the kitchen. Jay stood near the swinging doors while Ty walked around checking things out. Roland stood in the far corner of the kitchen, intently watching Ty. The ghost did not look happy; Jay was afraid that Roland would do something to scare the new prospective employee away. The ghost watched for a short while and then suddenly vanished. Jay breathed a huge sigh of relief.

"So, what do you think?"

"This is one great kitchen. You have appliances in here I have only seen in magazines. It would be an honor to work in this kitchen," Ty responded. "How big of a customer base are we talking a day?"

"There's twenty four-tops and ten eight-tops on the first floor. The second floor has the bar that seats twenty-four along with twenty more four-tops. That's two-hundred and forty diners on a busy night during the summer at any given time," Jay detailed.

"What are the hours of business?"

"Eleven to eleven," answered Jay. "Lunch and dinner."

"So, you are looking at two executive chefs, at least fourteen sous chefs, and ten prep cooks. Is that what you had figured?" Ty questioned.

"I was close. I figured twelve sous chefs, not fourteen. I hadn't even thought about prep cooks."

"You want one executive and at least seven sous on each shift. Plus, you need prep cooks constantly preparing the food the chefs need. This is quite a big operation."

"Have you ever opened a restaurant before? I mean from the very beginning?" Jay probed, impressed with the man in front of him.

"Yes, twice. I helped hire the staff, trained them, and ran the kitchen. It's all on my resume," answered Ty. "Have you had that many applicants?"

"Yes, there's a lot of people out there looking for jobs."

"Yes, that may be true, but are they qualified to do the work?" Ty challenged.

"The resumes look pretty impressive," Jay replied. "You are my first interview but I have four others who applied for the executive chef's positions."

"Do you mind if I take a look around?"

"No, just don't get in the way of the construction that's being done. We are on a tight schedule," Jay explained. "I'll be back at the table since the next applicant is due any minute."

"Great. I'll check in with you on the way out," Ty rejoined, heading off to explore the café.

Jay sat down pulling the next application out of the pile. Suddenly, Ty's paperwork flew off the table and landed on the floor. Jay looked around for Roland.

"I know you're here," Jay said, bending over to pick up the papers.

"Don't hire him…can't be trusted," Jay distinctly heard from behind him.

"You don't even know him. How do you know he can't be trusted?" he asked.

Before he could get an answer, a second person walked in for an interview. Jay repeated the process three more times. Ty still hadn't come back so Jay decided to go looking for him.

"Down cellar," Roland whispered in his ear. "I've been watching him."

"What the hell is he doing down cellar?" he asked Roland.

"Searching…" was the answer Jay received.

Jay entered the kitchen just as Ty came up from the cellar.

"That is one state-of-the-art wine locker you have downstairs," complimented Ty, smiling. "I've only seen one other one like it and that was down in Louisiana at a private plantation that I worked at. This place is a class act all the way."

"I thought you got lost," Jay questioned, frowning.

"Searching," murmured the ghost softly.

Apparently, Jay was the only one who heard the voice.

"No, I got to talking to some of the guys in the kitchen. They were saying this area would be done by this weekend," answered Ty, noticing Jay's displeasure that he was gone so long. "They told me to check out the wine locker down cellar."

"I'm heading out to lunch. I interviewed the other four while you were wandering around. I'll call you when I have made a decision. It should be within the next two days," Jay stated, dismissing Ty curtly.

"Sorry, Mr. Hallett. I didn't realize I was gone for that long. This place is beautiful and I would be honored to work here. I'll be looking forward to hearing from you," he said as he headed for the front door.

Jay watched him leave. He was, by far, the best candidate for lead executive chef. But, Jay couldn't shake the fact that for some reason, Roland didn't trust him. And why was he gone so long? This would take some serious consideration before Jay could make a final decision.

Robbie came in the door ready to interview the bartender applicants. Jay told him what he was looking for, the shift hours, and what was expected of them while they worked; the rest was up to Robbie. Jay could tell his younger brother was taking this seriously. Maybe, there was a chance he could step up and act like an adult after all. Time would tell.

Jay scooted out to The Burger Box for lunch. It was one of the few places in Anchor Point that stayed open year-round. Located on Main Street, it was owned by Cindy Nickerson of the Cape Cod Nickersons. Jay and Cindy had been in the same graduating class. They had dated their junior and senior year, but broke up when Jay went away to college, but they remained good friends to this day. Jay's Mom insisted that Cindy was the one for him. He always thought his Mom took it worse than he did when they had split up. He had to admit, he still had feelings for her, but the last time he was home visiting he found out she was engaged. It was way past time to move on.

Cindy was average in every way except her face; it was stunningly beautiful. Her most outstanding feature were her emerald green eyes. Right out of high school, she decided to try modeling. Turned out, it wasn't for her, and she returned to the Cape to run the family business.

He sat in the booth near the front window. Jay was an experienced people watcher. It was this talent that had given him an advantage in his law practice. Jay could learn a lot by watching a person and their actions. He also believed in first impressions. When he was younger he would sit on the town green and watch people for hours; it was a habit he had never lost.

"Well, look who's back. I do believe Mr. Jeremy Hallett has returned from the big city," Cindy stopped at his booth, smiling. "Are the rumors true?"

"Depends on what the rumors are," he answered, getting up to give her a big hug.

"Bea said you bought the lighthouse property and you are opening a café. How long have you been home?" asked Cindy as she sat down opposite him.

"A couple of months now. Those rumors are true; The Shipwreck Café will open June first. I'd love it if you and your fiancé would come to the grand opening. I'll save you the best table in the house," Jay promised.

"Is the offer still good if it's only me?" Cindy questioned, smiling shyly.

"What do you mean? Aren't you and Bill engaged anymore?" asked Jay with a glimmer of hope in his voice.

"No, I broke it off this past December. Things just weren't working in our relationship. Between you and me, he was too stuck up. Fun was not a word he could associate with," said Cindy in a low voice. "I think the word "boring" pretty well sums it up."

"I'm sorry it didn't work out for you," Jay commiserated.

"It's okay. I don't think my heart was really into the relationship from the very beginning."

"I'll tell you what," Jay proposed. "If you show up for the grand opening, I will still put you at the best table overlooking the ocean. I know the owner of the place, and I'm sure he would love to have dinner with you." He finished with a wiggle of his eyebrows.

"I would love to have dinner with the new owner. I can't wait to see what he has done with the property. What time should I be there?" she asked with a twinkle in her eye.

"Cindy, they need you out back for a delivery," interrupted one of the waitresses passing by the booth.

"I have to run. I can't wait for the first," said Cindy leaning in to give him a kiss on the cheek. "Could this be a real date after all these years?"

"I guess it is. I'll see you at seven for dinner," Jay's smile was blinding.

The waitress took Jay's food order. Enjoying his BLT, he watched Cindy rushing around taking care of any little thing that came up. He wondered if he would do that much running around once his place opened. He made a mental note to get one of those devices that registered his steps so he could keep track.

As he was finishing up his lunch, he heard a loud commotion outside the window where he was sitting. Tyrone Fenster was arguing with another guy almost twice his age. Suddenly, fists were flying along with loud words. The older man pinned the younger man against the window. Heated words were exchanged and the elder gentleman stalked away angrily. Ty hurried off in the opposite direction, not realizing that Jay had witnessed the entire event.

I wonder what that was all about? One more thing to add to the "con" list in hiring him.

Jay paid his bill and waved goodbye with a wink to Cindy.

He drove to the historical society to collect some more information on the lighthouse that would be printed on the front of the menus. The door was locked. It was supposed to be open, and it was well after Bea's lunch time, but she was nowhere to be found. Jay hoped she was okay. He looked through the front window and gasping at what he saw, pulled out his phone to call nine-one-one.

Chapter 6

JAY BANGED HEAVILY on the front door. He looked in the window again; the shoeless foot that was sticking out from behind the desk still hadn't moved. He ran around to the rear of the building to see if the back door was unlocked but it wasn't. Two police cars were pulling up to the front of the building as he ran back from the alley.

"I don't know if it's Bea Thomas or not," Jay panted out. "Someone is on lying the floor behind the desk."

Chief Stephen Boyd peered through the window.

"Nickerson, break down the door," he ordered sharply.

The sergeant put his shoulder to the door and it splintered with one hit. A crowd began to slowly gather on the adjacent sidewalk.

"Nickerson, keep everyone back. I don't want anyone within twenty feet of the building entrance," the Chief demanded.

Jay stood with Officer Tom Nickerson as the Chief cautiously entered the building. Tom was Cindy's younger brother and had been one year behind them in school. Jay and Tom had played varsity football together at Anchor Point High School while Cindy was a cheerleader. He had inherited the same green eyes his sister sported.

"Do you think it's Bea?" Jay whispered in concern.

Chief Boyd stepped to the front door and waved Jay and Tom into the building.

"It's Bea Thomas and she's dead. Tom, I need you to call the coroner. Tape off all around the building, including the back and the alley," he ordered.

"Do you think it was a heart attack?" Jay inquired.

"No. Don't go back there. It looks like someone took a bat to her head; it's not a pretty picture at all," answered Boyd. "Jay, did you see anyone around when you got here? She hasn't been dead very long; she's still warm."

"No, Stephen, I didn't."

"What were you doing here?" Tom questioned.

"I was here yesterday searching out information on the lighthouse," Jay responded, omitting the conversations they had discussed about treasure and ghosts. "I came back to research some more information for printing on the front of my menus for the café."

"Someone was definitely hunting for something specific," said the Chief, scratching his head. "This place is trashed; I wouldn't even begin to know if something has actually been removed."

"I can tell you one thing that's missing for sure," Jay offered up. "Pages have been ripped out of the guest book. Bea insisted that everyone who visited here sign the book. I autographed it yesterday when I was here and now that particular page is gone."

The Chief walked over to the small table holding the guest book. He put on latex gloves so he wouldn't smudge any existing fingerprints. He calculated how many pages were ripped out by the remnants left behind near the binding.

"Four pages are gone. It's picked clean all the way back to the beginning of this year," he said inserting the book into an evidence bag. "Off the top of your head, Jay, can you tell if anything else is missing?"

"It looks like several maps are gone from the rack next to the desk. Unless they have been thrown somewhere else in this mess," Jay responded, looking around in chagrin.

The coroner, Ed Nagle, and his assistant, Bobby Brown, arrived through the front door with a body bag and a gurney.

They wheeled it over to the body and closely examined the remains.

"The body's still warm," he confirmed. "She's been dead for less than an hour."

"That would be about right; Bea goes to lunch every day from noon to one. It's now two-twenty. She must have surprised whoever was here when she got back from eating or else they came in shortly after she returned to work," the Chief speculated.

"Who would do something like this to Bea? Everyone loved her," Ed questioned. "This was personal. Whoever it was, she knew this person. The first blow would have definitely killed her, but the rest was obviously uncontrollable rage. The blood spatter is widespread. Bobby, please take pictures of everything."

"So, what you are saying, Doc, is that this person should have been covered with blood as well when he left here?"

"Yes, he should have been enveloped in blood from head to toe," Ed responded seriously.

"Chief, there's some bloody shoe prints leading to the back door," Tom observed.

"Make sure we get plenty of pictures of them."

"Can we take the body now?" the coroner requested.

"Yea, we got all the pictures of Bea we need. Let me know what you find out as soon as possible," Boyd instructed.

The body was rolled over and carefully placed into the black bag.

"There's something in her hand," Jay noticed.

Boyd pried open Bea's hand and a small portion of a gold chain fell out. It was comprised of four separate links and was covered in blood.

"Nickerson, bag this. We need to determine if it belongs to Bea or the killer."

"I don't think it was Bea's, the links are too big. A rapper would wear a necklace that big, but not an elderly woman. It would be way too heavy for her. Besides, she didn't have any jewelry on yesterday when I was here, not even a ring," Jay remembered. "It doesn't look like she had any on today either."

"Maybe, the killer took her jewelry," Ed suggested.

"Maybe…" Boyd answered, looking around.

The coroner zipped up the bag and Bea left her life's work behind her for the very last time. The crowd out front had swelled to twice its original size. Some were crying while others were shaking their heads in disbelief. Cindy was standing in the crowd, waiting for her brother to come out and tell her what was going on.

"Jay, you can leave. We have work to do here. Be available if I need to talk to you," the Chief instructed. "Call me if you think of anything at all that might be helpful."

"Here's my business card with my cell phone number on it. I'll be at the lighthouse the rest of the week if you need me," Jay offered, following the gurney out the door.

"Jay, over here!" yelled Cindy, sticking her hand up in the air to be seen above the crowd.

Jay watched with grief as the body bag was being loaded into the coroner's wagon. He'd known Bea since he was a little boy; no one deserved to die the way she had. It made him furious that someone would attack a woman of her age so violently.

He ambled over to Cindy. The rest of the town people crowded around him to hear what he had to say. He felt like he was being suffocated as all the bodies pressed in.

"Was it Bea?" Cindy hesitantly asked.

"Yes, sadly, it was Bea. But I can't say anything more; you'll have to talk to Chief Boyd to get more details," Jay answered, looking at all the distraught faces.

"It's really bad, isn't it?' Cindy whispered.

"Come on," he said, grabbing her hand. "Do you have to get right back to work?"

"No, I'm done for the day," she replied.

They climbed into Jay's car and drove to the picnic area located near the point. Jay stepped out and sat down on one of the picnic tables. He buried his face in his hands and cried as Cindy vaulted up next to him.

"It wasn't natural causes, was it?" she asked as she put her arm around his shoulders to comfort him.

"It was horrible, Cindy. I don't understand how one human being could do something sickening like that to another human being."

"There are some real sick whackos in this world, unfortunately. I didn't think we had anyone like that in Anchor Point though," Cindy said sadly. "With the influx of tourists that we get, it could have been anyone."

"The Doc said he thought it was someone she knew. He said the rage looked like it was personal. I wish I had looked around more carefully when I saw her on the floor through the door," Jay regretted. "I should have been more alert."

"You didn't know what had happened inside. She was already dead and you couldn't have changed that," Cindy comforted, trying to reassure her friend.

"I wish I had paid more attention to the guest book when I signed it yesterday. Whoever the killer was, he must have signed the book within the last five months," Jay confided, thinking out loud.

"Why do you say that?"

"Four pages had been torn out. Perhaps the killer could have been in there more than once. He ripped out the pages that went back to the beginning of this year," Jay observed.

"Weird. What could be so important inside a historical society to kill for?" Cindy pondered.

"I don't know, but I'm going to find out," Jay stated determinately. "I need to check in with my brother and see how the interviews are going. Want to come along?"

"Sure, I'd love to."

They drove cautiously up the hill to the lighthouse parking lot. The workers were hastily packing up for the day. The foreman spoke briefly to Jay to update him on the progress of the renovations.

"Jeez, I haven't been here since I was a little kid," said Cindy in wonder as they entered the cafe. "Since that night…"

"Since what night?" asked Jay, holding the door open.

"Oh, never mind. This place looks phenomenal," she said, looking around. "I can't believe this used to be all empty space."

"Classy, huh?" asked Jay proudly.

"Hey, big brother," yelled Robbie over the balcony. "Interviews are done and I hired eight people today. Are you coming up?"

"I'll be right there. Come check out the upstairs. The windows are in and it's an awesome sight," said Jay, taking her hand.

"Hey, Cindy. What's up?" asked Robbie as they hit the top stair.

"How'd everything go?" Jay inquired.

"I hired everyone that showed up except one guy. He smelled like booze. I was afraid he'd drink up the profits. The others I put in a tentative schedule according to what hours they would be available," said Robbie handing the application packets over to his brother along with the schedule.

"This looks great. Does this mean I don't have to do the scheduling for the bar personnel?" Jay questioned.

"No problem, I can do it," said Robbie with a grin. "Isn't that part of the manager's duties?"

"I guess you're right. From now on, it's your job."

"J…a…y" Cindy sang out, her hands clawing the air to reach Jay's arm.

"Cindy, what's wrong?" he asked looking at her face in surprise.

Jay turned to look where she was staring; Roland was

standing right there.

"I'm not crazy. After all these years, he's really here," stammered Cindy. "I did see him that night."

"What night?" asked Jay, ignoring the ghost.

"One evening a group of us came up here treasure hunting. I was poking around in the base of the lighthouse when this creepy feeling came over me and I felt that someone was watching me. I looked up at the spiral stairs and a guy wearing a black coat pointed his finger towards me and ordered me to get out. The stairs were visible right through his body. I let out a scream and ran all the way down to the main road with everyone chasing me," said Cindy as she stared at Roland in dismay.

"Who's here? Don't tell me the ghost is here. How come you can see him and I can't?" Robbie groused, looking around. "Where is he?"

Robbie could hear footsteps echoing and the hair stood straight up on his arms. Roland floated mistily over to where Cindy stood.

"I remember you…" he said as he vanished.

"Where is he?" insisted Robbie.

"He's gone," answered Jay.

"You can see him, too? This so sucks," Robbie said indignantly.

"This place really is haunted. What a great business angle for your café," Cindy suggested, smiling. "Come have dinner with a ghost."

"We're not going to say anything about the ghosts," Jay grumbled.

"Ghosts, plural? There's more than one?" asked Robbie. "You didn't tell me that when I took the job."

"Seriously? There's more than one? This gets better by the minute," Cindy said excitedly.

"Roland won't bother you, Robbie. He'll hide out in the lighthouse while the café is open since he doesn't like the noise.

Colleen is a ten-year-old girl who was lost in the wreck of The Fallen Mist. She stays out on the point looking for her mother," Jay confided sadly.

"And you've seen both?" asked Cindy in amazement.

"Yes, I have. I've talked to Roland several times," Jay responded. "Bea was the one who gave me all the information on this place. She also admonished me to keep it quiet. She said bringing up the ghosts would remind people of the hidden treasure story."

"I'd forgotten about the treasure after that night," Cindy remembered.

"Bea said if it was brought to people's attention again, I would have treasure hunters digging everywhere on my property," said Jay, shaking his head. "I don't want that and I'm positive Roland doesn't either."

"Wait a minute, what treasure?" asked Robbie. "You are so holding out on me, Jay."

"Mr. Hallett, can I speak to you for a minute before I leave?" asked the kitchen foreman.

"Cindy, will you tell my brother the story about the Knowles treasure? I'll be right back."

Twenty minutes later Jay, walked back to Cindy and Robbie. A member of the Board of Health had come by to see the progress of the kitchen and set up a date for the final inspection. The following Wednesday at two in the afternoon was scheduled. Jay would have his executive chefs in place this weekend so they could make certain that the kitchen was ready for business.

He finished Cindy's tour with the final stop being the table that they would have dinner at on the night of the grand opening. They stood together, looking out over the ocean through the newly installed panoramic windows.

"It's breathtaking," Cindy whispered in awe. "I can't believe how gorgeous this place is and what all you have done with it."

"I'm proud of the place," Jay responded, beaming. "But, I don't think Roland likes the changes at all."

"What are you going to do if people see him? It could be good for business, but bad for privacy," Cindy inquired.

"I suggested to him that he should stay up in the lighthouse until the café closes at night. I don't know if he'll listen, so we'll have to wait and see," Jay confided.

"What about staff?" Cindy asked curiously.

"Interviews will be finished tomorrow and training begins on Monday," answered Jay. "We should be ready to rock the following week for the grand opening."

"I can't wait," Cindy stated with excitement.

"Jay, I have the first liquor order being delivered tomorrow. Will you be around?" Robbie interrupted.

"What's the matter? Don't want to be up here by yourself with the big, bad ghost?" Jay teased.

"Not funny. I promised I'd take Mom to the doctor's tomorrow. I just want to make sure someone will be here in case I'm not," answered Robbie, throwing a balled-up bar napkin at his brother.

"Is she okay?" Jay asked in concern.

"Yea, she's fine. Just a final check-up before she heads off to Florida."

"Yea, I'll be here all day. Final day of interviews."

"Okay, I'm gone. Going to get an hour of surfing in before it gets too dark," said Robbie. "See you in the morning. Bye, Cindy. It was nice to see you again."

"You, too."

The couple walked downstairs and the place echoed eerily since the workers had gone for the day.

"I'll lock up and take you back to your car," Jay offered, shutting out the lights.

"Jay, who do you think killed Bea?" asked Cindy as they walked to the car. "She was such a sweet old lady."

"I don't know. Maybe they'll have some theories when they figure out exactly what was taken. Whoever it was knew Bea and got pretty pissed off when she apparently wouldn't help them," stated Jay. "Just be careful; please don't go anywhere by yourself until they catch whoever did this."

"I won't. I'm not taking any chances on missing out on our dinner under the stars," she answered, smiling.

Jay grinned like a loon. While he was dating in Boston, Cindy had never left his mind or his heart. He would never admit it to her, but his mother was probably right. Her son and Cindy really did belong together.

They drove back to her car at The Burger Box in comfortable silence. He watched carefully until she was safely inside and her car doors were locked. Watching her drive away, he smiled in anticipation of what the future might bring. He was home and Cindy was apparently in his life again.

Jay arrived shortly at cottage. Stormy pranced around him, happy to see him finally home. Opening the refrigerator, he pushed around several bottles of beer, and picked out one of the new flavors of beer the salesman had given him to try. Stormy gulped down her supper and then laid sprawled out on the couch next to Jay as he ate his. Jay racked his brain trying to remember the other names that were located near his signature in the guest book. At the time, it just hadn't seemed that important.

He was obviously losing his edge as an attorney. Six months ago, he would have looked over the details of the book as he signed it. Six months ago, he would have surveyed the entire area around the historical society once he saw the body on the floor. God knew, he thought he had seen everything. Gory pictures had never bothered him before, but this time the victim was a long-time friend. This time, it was different. The only saving grace was that she hadn't suffered. He felt the tears welling up again as he remembered the sweet old lady he had known all his life.

As he climbed the stairs wearily, the dog followed him upstairs to bed.

"I'm really glad you're here with me tonight, Stormy," he said, hugging the dog. "Please don't leave me, okay?"

She looked at him steadily, tilting her head sideways. Jay fluffed his pillow and laid down on the comfy bed. Stormy settled in, snuggling against Jay's body, softly placing her head on the corner of his pillow. They both closed their eyes in exhaustion and slept peacefully together through the long night.

The rest of the week seemed to pass in a blur. Interviews, deliveries, and final preparations were now in full swing. Phone calls were made to the applicants who had secured jobs; training would begin for them Monday morning. The new computer system had been installed and was up and running. Appliances were finally in place, two dishwashers had been hooked up in the dish room, and the wine locker was chilling a new stock of varying wines.

Fighting the negative feeling deep in his gut, Jay decided to hire Tyrone as the lead executive chef. He knew how to open a restaurant and Jay needed someone like that in his kitchen for the start-up. The attorney in him was saying Ty would be trouble down the road, but the businessman in him was saying he's the one I need to hire for now.

He asked him to come in on Saturday to meet the other executive chef that he would be working with. Susan Myers was the new employee hired as second in charge in the kitchen.

The three of them would sit down and finalize the menu so Jay could send it off to the printer. He had already called Tinneys, the local printer, to make sure that a rush job would be feasible. He needed the finished menus back by Wednesday as the grand opening was only three days later.

After Saturday, the kitchen would be turned over to the experienced hands of Ty and Susan. It would be their responsibility to have everything in order and ready to go on opening night. Jay would check in with them every day to see what else was needed and what still had to be done.

Jay chose Mary Chase, one of the fourteen sous chefs that had been hired, to be the one person who would be trusted with his mother's secret chowder recipe. Mary was in her mid-thirties, a single woman, and very shy. If a person was asked to describe her appearance, the words "spinster librarian" would come to mind.

It would be her responsibility to come in every morning to prepare the clam chowder fresh for that day's business. She acknowledged that it would be a seven-day-a-week job with the hours being seven in the morning until noon. Because she was working every day her pay would be slightly higher than the other sous chefs that didn't.

Monday morning, the trainees arrived bright-eyed and ready to learn. Jay worked with the hostesses and waitresses while Robbie trained the bartenders. Ty could be heard in the kitchen barking orders to the sous chefs and prep cooks as the deliveries poured in all day long. Half of the waitresses had been put to work setting up the tables while the other half trained on the computers and then they switched off.

Jay was working with the three hostesses that he had hired when his Mom waltzed through the front door. She halted in place, looking around in stunned amazement.

"Jay, this place is sensational!" she applauded, walking towards him.

"Hi, Mom," Robbie threw out as he headed to the elevator with full boxes of booze on the dolly.

"Hello, son. Aren't you the busy one?" she acknowledged. "Jay, do you have a minute?"

"What's up, Mom?" he asked, kissing her on the cheek.

"I have a problem and I was hoping you could help me with it."

"Are you okay? I know you went to the doctors last week,"

asked Jay, concerned for his mother.

"My health is fine," she assured him. "I have a more pressing problem."

"Anything, Mom. What do you need?"

"Theresa can't go to Florida right now. Her daughter has just been diagnosed with breast cancer, so she needs to stay here and move in with her to help take care of the kids. My house is already sold, and I'm staying at Grampa's cottage for now," she said, sighing. "The problem is, I gave up my job at the beauty parlor and they have already hired someone to replace me."

"You need me to pay the rent? I can do that," Jay offered immediately.

"No, I can handle the rent from the sale of the house. What I need is a job. I can't sit around and do nothing until Theresa is free to move. We had decided to buy a house together and I don't want to proceed without her being there."

"Hmm, you're up early every day, right?" Jay asked.

"Five-thirty every morning," she answered, beaming.

"I have the perfect job for you. We're serving your famous homemade chowder. I have entrusted only one person with the recipe. How would you like to come in each morning and team up with her to prepare it?"

"Are you making this up just to give your old mother a job?" Martha hesitated.

"No, actually, it's helping me out. I hired Mary Chase for seven days a week. If you work with her, I can arrange a schedule for each of you to have a day or two off."

"I know Mary; quiet young lady. I would love to work with her," his Mom responded.

"Great. I have asked her to come in Friday morning to do a dry run on a first batch. Can you be here then?"

"I'll be here with bells on!" his Mom answered with a devilish grin.

"Wonderful! I have to run. The video is over for the

computer training. Time to have them enter orders in the training mode," said Jay hugging his Mom with excitement. "I'll see you on Friday then."

The rest of the week passed in a blur of activity for Jay and Robbie. Everything seemed to come together like it was supposed to for the grand opening. Finally, Friday night had arrived and everyone had gone home for the day. Jay walked around the restaurant checking every little final detail. The Shipwreck Cafe was completely ready to open for business.

Standing behind the bar, he poured himself a Crown Royal on the rocks. He held the glass in the air and toasted to his new life and to the upcoming success of his new restaurant. Roland materialized suddenly at the edge of the bar.

"I wish I could serve you a drink, my friend," Jay offered the ghost with a smile.

Roland nodded his head sagely and then vanished. Jay was left alone to enjoy his drink, looking out over the undulating ocean.

Chapter 7

IT WAS FINALLY grand opening day. Jay couldn't sleep, so at five in the morning he and Stormy were down running the beach below the point. The ghost of Colleen was watching the dog from above the cliffs. Jay waved to her and as usual, she vanished.

He found himself studying the underside of the cliffs. If there were more caves and hidden treasures, he now owned it all. His thoughts returned to Roland Knowles and the treasure he had supposedly hidden. Was it still on the property? Did it belong to Jay if he found it or would he have to turn it over to Roland's relatives? He had so many unanswered questions.

Jay dropped down in the sand, watching his dog run in and out of the surf. Stormy seemed truly happy now; she had a permanent home and loved Jay just as much as he loved her. He didn't have to keep her on her leash anymore in fear that she would run away. She never strayed far from her owner, always keeping him in sight. Stormy galloped up to him, planted her feet, and shook all over. Jay was suddenly covered with sand and salt water everywhere.

"Good thing I'm going to take a shower," he said laughing, hugging the dog. "Come on, girl. Let's head home."

While Stormy bolted down her breakfast, Jay shaved and cleaned up in the shower. He pulled the new, dark grey, pinstriped suit he had bought for the opening out of the closet. Getting dressed, he looked in the mirror to be certain his tie was on straight. Staring back at him was the image of the attorney he had left behind in Boston. Jay decided he didn't like that image; after today, it would be Dockers and polo shirts every day. Five star food served in a comfortable setting would be Jay's ultimate goal for The Shipwreck Café.

"I think we're finally ready," he commented to the dog who was sitting next to him.

It was eight o'clock and they headed out for the café. Stormy automatically followed Jay into the building. As they entered, the dog sat down just inside the door, growling. Jay looked around for Roland; he was standing next to the door that connected to the lighthouse.

"Today's opening day, Roland. You might want to stay up in the lighthouse. It's going to be busy and noisy," he informed the ghost.

"Who are you talking to?" his mom asked, coming out of the kitchen.

Jay watched Roland walk through the solid door.

"Just talking to Stormy," he answered. "Is the chowder finally ready?"

"Triple batches, ready to go. I love working with Mary, she's so laid back," she answered, giving her son a tight hug.

"I'm glad you're still here to share this with me," he confided, smiling and hugging her back.

"I am so proud of you, Jay. Your brother, too. I just can't believe he finally has a full-time job. And this place… this place is beautiful," she complimented, smiling. "Have you seen Roland yet?"

"Excuse me?" Jay braked to a halt, not believing what she had just asked him.

"He was in the kitchen watching me when I got here early this morning. Mary didn't seem to see him, but I did. I smiled at him and he disappeared," she said matter-of-factly. "That's who you were talking to, right?"

"Mom, whatever you do, don't tell Robbie you can see

Roland. He'll freak. It's like he's the only one around here that can't see him," Jay cautioned.

"I won't say a word," she promised. "I'm heading back to the kitchen."

Jay took Stormy to his office where she had toys, treats, and a comfy over-stuffed bed waiting for her. He didn't want to leave her by herself all day long at the cottage. This way, he could sneak off, take her outside to do her business, and spend a few minutes alone with her. He didn't want Stormy to feel neglected because the café was opening for business. He knew he had to balance his time for both. He watched as the dog settled down comfortably on her bed.

The kitchen was now crazy with activity. Steam tables had been filled to capacity, dishes were stacked neatly according to size, and pans full of boiling water ready for lobsters were on the stoves. Chefs in their crisp, clean whites were scurrying around the kitchen completing last minute preparations and Ty was yelling at one of the younger sous chefs. Jay would have to be sure and speak to him later about the way he treated the other chefs.

Jay sashayed back to the front door. He made sure the menus were ready for the hostesses and that the computer system was online and ready for orders. He walked both floors, checking the nine computer screens to make sure they were on and working. He stood near the windows, feeling small when compared to the ocean and its power. His eyes looked upwards.

"Dad, I miss you. I know Robbie does, too. Mom's here with me today. I'm so happy and relieved she decided to stay here for awhile. I hope you're looking down seeing how wonderful this place is and how it's brought us all together again. I really wish you were here with us," whispered Jay, tearing up. "I know you wanted me to be an attorney, but I just couldn't do it anymore after that girl lost her life because I twisted the law for a rich person and his money. I took the money I made from that case and turned it into something good, Dad. I've provided jobs for a lot of people here. I hope you won't be too disappointed in me."

He sensed a hand on his shoulder; Roland was standing next to him.

"He's very proud of you," Roland said.

They stood there together for several seconds in silence. Robbie came bounding up the stairs yelling for his brother, and Jay sensed the ghost disappear.

"Jay, you need to come downstairs. Timmy from the florist shop is here with the floral deliveries. There are so many deliveries, I don't know where to put them all," Robbie said, pulling on his brother's arm.

Flower arrangements, potted trees, and a variety of terrariums were brought in from the truck. Jay and Robbie positioned them in the entrance and the waiting area. Each was accompanied by a card wishing them good luck at their new opening. Almost every business in town had wished The Shipwreck Café much success.

The staff started to arrive steadily. It was ten-thirty and the café would be open for business in just half an hour. Cars were already pulling into the parking lot. Jay assembled the staff together at the bar. Robbie had poured champagne; everyone took a glass for a toast.

"I want to thank everyone for the great job of working together to get this place open on time. I know there probably will be glitches here and there during today and tonight. It's to be expected. Hopefully, lunch will be a little slower than dinner tonight so we can smooth out the rough patches. I would like everyone to raise their glass now in a toast to Bea Thomas. She knew everyone in town and everyone loved her. I promised her a drink when she came to dinner tonight, so this is for her."

"To Bea," said the group, raising their glasses in the air.

"Now, let's open this sucker up," said Jay with a huge grin

on his face.

The staff took up their positions. Jay checked on Stormy one more time before he unlocked the front door to a throng of people. He stepped outside and grabbed hold of the red ribbon that was stretched across the front door. His Mom and brother stood behind him smiling proudly.

The local newspaper was covering the opening. Gabe Fulton, the lead reporter for the paper was snapping pictures of the family. Gabe had graduated with Robbie; they were surf buddies and still partied together.

"Welcome to The Shipwreck Café. My name is Jeremy Hallett, most of you call me Jay, and I am the new owner. I hope you enjoy your visit here. If you step in to the waiting area our two hostesses will seat you as quickly as possible. Again, welcome to our grand opening."

He pulled a pair of scissors out of his suitcoat pocket and cut the ribbon. A loud cheer went up from the crowd. Robbie disappeared inside. His Mom stayed out front to talk the locals who had come for lunch.

Jay stayed just inside the door greeting customers as they entered, guiding them to the waiting area. The hostesses took over from there, seating them in a rotating system between sections. He noticed that most of the customers were tourists. Jay assumed the locals were working and would come in for dinner tonight instead.

The reporter walked around snapping multiple pictures of the interior of the restaurant. He returned from the second floor and walked directly over to Jay.

"I snapped enough pictures for the paper. Can I take a couple of pictures of the menu while I eat lunch?" he asked.

"Sure," Jay answered. "Lunch is on me; tell your waitress I said so. Just leave her a good tip."

"Thanks, Jay. This story will run on the front-page tomorrow. I'm going to sit at the bar with Robbie. Is that okay?"

"Sure. Spy on him and let me know how he is doing on your way out," said Jay laughing.

Memorial Weekend signaled the beginning of tourist season for the Cape. Lunch was steady, but not overwhelming. A few small problems cropped up, but were taken care of quickly. Martha came out of the kitchen around one o'clock and she found Jay standing at the register talking to Chief Boyd. He was looking very serious and Jay did not look happy listening to him.

"Hello, Stephen. Are you here for lunch?" asked Martha.

"I'm afraid not. I'm here on official business. I'll be here for supper later, though. Would you like to dine with me and the Mrs.?"

"Thank you for the invitation, but I'm going to be eating with Theresa later. Sorry," answered Jay's Mom.

"Jay tells me you're working here," said the Chief. "I also heard this fine establishment is serving the best clam chowder on Cape Cod. Please, tell me it's your recipe, Martha."

"Yes, it is. Speaking of chowder, Jay, we have a small problem. Mary left at noon and the chowder is almost half gone. Do you want me stay and make another triple batch?" asked Martha. "You won't have enough for tonight if I don't."

"Would you mind, Mom? I can't run out of our signature chowder on the very first night."

"Anything for my son," she said, smiling. "You spent too much time in Boston. It's not chowder, it's chowdah. Your Dad used to correct the tourists all the time. "AH," he would tell them."

"Your Mom is classic," chuckled Boyd watching her walk back to the kitchen.

"So, are you sure the only things missing out of the historical society are three maps of this property?" Jay inquired.

"There was a small safe in the back room that had its contents emptied also. We don't know what was in it," answered the Chief. "The volunteers who worked with Bea said she was the only one who knew what was in the safe."

"Do you think she opened it for whoever killed her?" asked Jay.

"We don't know," answered Boyd. "Just be careful, Jay. We don't know why they took only those maps, but common sense says it has something to do with the Knowles treasure."

"Great. Bea warned me to keep quiet about the place being haunted. She said if the Knowles name was brought up it would bring the treasure hunters in droves to the property. It looks like it may have already started," said Jay shaking his head. "And poor Bea got caught in the crossfire."

"I'll keep you updated," said Boyd. "See you for dinner tonight."

Jay called the head hostess, Kathy Julin, over to man the front door while he took a break to take Stormy out. Then he was going to check on the kitchen staff and Robbie at the bar before he came back.

"Go, we've slowed down enough that I am going to start breaks for the waitresses. I'll call you if I need anything," she said, taking the menus from his hands.

Stormy was ready to stretch her legs. He took her out the back door that led to the lighthouse. He walked around, inhaling the fresh salt air while the dog ran around joyfully. Jay shielded his eyes against the sun to look over the lighthouse structure and realized it needed a good coat of paint. Looking up at the catwalk, he saw Roland looking back down at him. Jay hoped no one else would spot him manning his post. He couldn't very well say anything to the ghost because that's where Jay had told him to go while the café was open.

Jay returned the dog to his office and gave her a new pig's ear to chew on as a reward for being so good. Checking in with Robbie, he learned everything had gone smoothly at the bar. The real test would be tonight.

As Jay entered the kitchen, he heard Ty yelling at several of the prep cooks. Susan walked by him, frowning and shaking her head in disgust, so Jay followed her into the executive chef's office.

"Tell me what you're thinking, Susan," Jay asked.

"Do you really want to know what I'm thinking?" she asked, looking at the door.

"Yes," answered Jay, walking over to close the door.

"Fine. Ty is a bully. He does not know how to work with people, only over them. He has screamed at everyone in the kitchen, belittling them. He reduced one of the prep cook to tears and she quit and walked out. Everyone here hates him and it's only the first day. If this keeps up, you'll have no staff left to man the kitchen," said Susan.

"What about you? How has he treated you?" asked Jay.

"Terrible. He's embarrassed me in front of the line. He informed all the sous chefs that I have no idea what I am doing and the title of executive chef should be reserved for people who deserve the title," Susan exclaimed, slamming her fist down on the desk. "I graduated the top of my class; I am more than qualified for this job. As a matter of fact, I am more qualified for his job than he is."

"Do your best to get through your shift today. I will have a serious talk with him and things will be different tomorrow, I promise. Please get me the name of the girl who quit. I need to call her and get her back here," Jay requested.

He left Susan looking for the paperwork of the prep cook who had quit. When Jay came out of the office, he noticed Ty glaring in Susan's direction. The chef then realized his boss was staring at him and quickly pulled out his pocket watch, checked the time, and yelled at the kitchen staff that it was one hour until the supper rush began. Jay walked over to his Mom who was just finishing up the last batch of clam chowder.

"Has Ty yelled at you, Mom?" whispered Jay.

"He wouldn't dare," she answered defiantly. "But, he's

yelled at everyone else."

"I just heard. Things will change. I just need to get through the opening tonight."

"I hope so. He's brutal, thinks he's better than everyone else," said his Mom stirring the chowder. "In my opinion, you'd be better off without him. Everyone loves Susan and she definitely knows how to run a kitchen."

"Thanks, Mom," said Jay kissing her on the cheek. "I have to get back out front."

"I'll take Stormy out before it gets too dark. I'm almost finished here."

"Love you. You're the best," said Jay.

"I know," she said, smiling in contentment.

Ty watched to make sure Jay left the kitchen, then he went to the office and closed the door. A verbal fight broke out between Susan and Ty that the rest of the kitchen staff watched through the glass windows. Martha didn't like how close Ty was standing to his second in command. She bravely walked over to the office and rapped loudly on the door.

"Susan, you're needed on the line. Orders are backing up," Martha interrupted.

Susan grabbed her head covering and angrily brushed by Ty. Fire in his eyes, he turned to say something to Martha.

"Don't even," she said as she walked away. "Pompous putz."

Martha watched Ty out of the corner of her eye. He punched the filing cabinet and slammed the office door closed. Sitting at his desk, he stared at Martha, who stared right back. He didn't like someone undermining his authority, especially an old lady. He'd put her in her place. Maybe not today, but soon.

The kitchen was cranking out dinners. Things were running smoothly without Ty around. Opening night was going to prove to be busier than even Jay had hoped. Martha left one of the containers of chowder on the prep table next to the steam table and she had one of the prep cooks put the other two in the walk-in.

Stormy met her at the door, tail wagging. Martha took her canine friend out to do her business. She kept her on a leash because she didn't want the dog running out in front of a car coming up the hill. Stormy just wasn't used to this volume of traffic around her house.

She used her son's private bathroom in the office to clean up and change. Theresa would meet her at six-thirty for supper and they were going to eat upstairs near the windows overlooking the ocean. Martha had a half an hour to relax; she fed the dog her supper and stretched out on the couch. In the middle of eating, Stormy lifted her head and growled; Roland was standing in the corner of the office.

"Hello, Roland," said Martha. "I thought you'd be up in the lighthouse."

Stormy continued to growl.

"It's okay, Stormy. Eat your supper," she said, turning to the ghost again. "You be good to my boys, you hear? They're good kids."

Roland smiled. He was impressed that the woman wasn't the least bit afraid of him. Martha could hear words being spoken, but the ghost's lips weren't moving.

"Watch the cook. Not to be trusted."

"I know. I don't like him much either. Jay will set him straight, don't you worry," she assured the ghost. "If I have my way, he'll be gone and Susan will oversee the kitchen."

"He thinks because he's family, he can find the treasure," said Roland. "He never will."

"Are you saying the treasure is still here?" asked Martha in surprise.

"Maybe," answered the ghost, smiling.

"Please, don't tell anyone that. Jay is afraid that people will overrun the property in search of it. He's afraid the point will be destroyed. Let it stay buried," said Martha.

"For you, I will be quiet," said Roland, walking through the door to the lighthouse.

She gave Stormy a treat and told her to lay down and be good. The dog walked to her bed and did as she was told. Her eyes were closed in sleep before Martha even left the office.

The restaurant was filled with smiling customers and the waiting area was also full. People sat sipping drinks waiting for their name to be called. A large percentage of the tables held locals who had come out to support Jay. He stood at the door, smiling his "to die for" smile, receiving hugs and handshakes from all the patrons who entered.

Theresa was waiting at the hostess station for Martha. Jay took one lady on each arm and escorted them upstairs. They stopped at the bar to say hi to Robbie who was buried elbow deep in slips ordering drinks for the dining room. Peter was serving the rest of the people seated around the bar. The tip glasses were overflowing; Robbie and Peter were having a great night.

In the far corner of the room, a small section had been roped off for private use. Three tables sat waiting for their special patrons to arrive; these were the best seats in the house. Jay's Mom and friend would be seated at one of the tables, the second was reserved for Jay and Cindy.

The third table had been set with a single place setting. A white rose in a crystal vase had been placed next to a glass of red wine. A place card stood in the center of the plate that read *In Memory of Bea.*

Jay sat the ladies at their table.

"Son, this view is stunning," said Martha, looking out the window. "These windows were the best idea you had."

"Everything is on the house tonight, for both of you," insisted Jay. "Order whatever you want and don't worry about the cost."

"I know one thing I'm not ordering," said Martha, laughing. "No chowder for me."

"I'll be back up shortly with Cindy. I'm going to celebrate by having dinner in my own place," said Jay, waiting for his mother to say something about Cindy.

"See, I told you so," his Mom whispered to Theresa.

"I have to make the rounds and make sure everything's okay before I finally sit down for dinner."

"Check the kitchen. I don't like that Ty fella and neither does you know who. We don't trust him," said Martha placing her napkin in her lap.

"That's where I'm heading first," assured her son.

The kitchen was going nonstop. The computer screens were filled with orders and the chefs were getting the food out as fast as they possibly could. Susan was out on the front line, but there was no sign of Ty.

"Susan, everything okay?"

She nodded.

"Where's Ty?" Jay questioned.

"I don't know," she said, with a shrug. "He disappeared a while ago. Jamie, I need a side of sweet potato fries."

Jay looked around the kitchen but Ty was nowhere to be seen and the office was empty. Before he could investigate any further where his missing chef was, Kathy came through the kitchen doors.

"Jay, we need you out front," she said.

"Susan, can you handle this without Ty?" asked Jay.

"Not a problem, boss. We have a great team in place. We don't need him. He causes more confusion than calm when he's here," she answered. "ORDER UP!"

Jay arrived at the hostess station to see Kathy arguing with a couple.

"Is there a problem here?" asked Jay, sticking out his hand. "I'm Jay Hallett, the owner."

"Your hostess is not being very accommodating," complained the woman.

Jay looked at Kathy for an explanation.

"Boss, they were seated at the bar waiting for a table. They saw Bea's empty table and demanded to be seated there. I tried to explain to them why the table was empty, but they didn't want to listen," Kathy explained.

"That's one of the stupidest things I have ever heard. Saving a table for someone who's dead, what a waste of space," grumbled the woman. "You wouldn't see something like that in the city."

"Obviously, you are not from around here and this is not the city. Bea Thomas was brutally murdered at her place of work this week. She was born and raised here and loved by everyone. That table is reserved for Bea and no one else. I'm sorry if you can't understand that," Jay patiently informed them.

"Come on, Raymond," she said, turning for the door. "We'll find somewhere else to eat. And, we're not paying for the drinks we had; we waited too long as it was."

She marched out the door as her husband turned to Jay.

"I'm sorry about your friend. My wife can be terribly rude sometimes. Good luck with your business," he said tucking some money into Jay's hand. "This is for the drinks. Stick the rest in the bar tip jar. Again, I'm really sorry."

Jay took the money upstairs. He found out from Peter that the couple had only been sitting at the bar about ten minutes. After five minutes, the woman started complaining about not being seated. They had two drinks and the total tab was only fourteen dollars.

"The husband felt bad for you guys," said Jay holding out a hundred-dollar bill. "Pay for the two drinks and give me a twenty for Kathy. She took the brunt of that woman's insults. The rest goes to you and Robbie."

"Nice," said Peter, handing Jay a twenty.

Cindy had been sitting in the waiting area drinking a glass of white wine. She was wearing a light green dress that made her green eyes pop. Her hair had been swept up in the back and held in place with a crystal clip. She smiled as soon as she spotted Jay.

Jay handed Kathy the twenty.

"It's an apology from her husband," explained Jay. "I'm going up to have dinner with Cindy. Are you okay here by yourself? I'll cover for you when I get back."

"Go. Celebrate. We'll be fine."

Jay took Cindy's arm and led her upstairs. She said "hi" to Martha and Theresa, giving them each a hug. As promised, the couple sat down at the best table in the house. For the next hour, Jay was lost in his time with Cindy. They caught up on each other's lives while eating baked stuffed lobsters. A bottle of champagne was presented to Jay as a surprise from his brother. Before Jay realized it, an hour and a half had passed.

"Cindy, I have to get back downstairs. I'm sorry it must be so rushed tonight. Next time, I won't be working," said Jay, standing up.

"Next time? Does that mean we're going to have a second date?" she asked, smiling hopefully.

"You bet it does," said Jay, giving her a quick kiss.

"I'll see my own way out. There's a few people I need to say "hi" to," said Cindy. "I think the whole town is here."

Jay gave Robbie a holler as he walked by and Robbie returned a thumb's up. He decided to go down the waitresses' elevator and enter the kitchen from the back. He wanted to observe the staff in action, especially Ty, without his being seen. Again, the head executive chef was nowhere to be seen. Jay was pissed; he walked through the kitchen, stopping in front of Susan.

"Where's Ty?" he asked.

"Don't know, boss. He hasn't been here most of the night,"

she answered.

"Everything going okay?"

"A few problems here and there. Nothing we all couldn't take care of together," said Susan, setting finished dinners up under the heat lamps.

"I think I am looking at my new first executive chef," whispered Jay, leaning in so only Susan would hear. "Just don't say anything until I fire TY."

Susan smiled. "Whatever you say, boss."

Jay closed the doors on his first day of business at ten p.m. The bar stayed open until eleven to accommodate the patrons still eating. Kathy stationed herself at the front door to let people out, but no new customers in as the kitchen closed at ten.

Jay was happily exhausted; the place had been filled to capacity all night. The whole town had attended his opening. It was a great feeling to be back home amongst friends and family.

Now, he had the unpleasant task of firing Ty; this was not going to be easy. The chef had a temper and Jay didn't want to be on the receiving end of it. But as the owner, this was one of those unpleasant things that came with the title.

He entered the kitchen as Susan and one other sous chef were finishing up. The whole area had been cleaned and reset for the next day's business.

"Phenomenal job, Susan," said Jay shaking her hand. "Where's Ty?

"He showed up from God knows where about an hour and a half ago. He grabbed something to eat and said he was going to the office to order produce for tomorrow. I think he's still there," she informed him.

"Again, great job. I'll see you tomorrow. You too, Josh," said Jay, heading to the office.

The owner looked through the window and saw Ty was facing the computer, his back to the door. The produce inventory sheet was up on the screen. Jay knocked, but got no response so he entered the office. A half-eaten bowl of clam chowder sat on the desk. A spoon, dripping with chowder residue was lying on the floor next to the chef's chair.

Jay felt for a pulse. Ty was dead.

Chapter 8

"SUSAN, CALL NINE-ONE-ONE," yelled Jay. "Tell them to send the police, too."

Jay stood outside the office guarding the door. He didn't want anything tampered with before Boyd arrived. He could see Susan on the phone; Josh was staring at his boss trying to figure out what was going on.

"Josh, please go out and wait at the front door for the ambulance. When they get here, show them to the office," requested Jay.

"Sure, boss. No problem," he answered.

Jay started pacing back and forth. He couldn't believe something like this was happening on opening night. Did his mother's chowder have anything to do with Ty's death? It couldn't have, hundreds of people had eaten chowder tonight from the same batch. He wished the Chief would hurry and get there.

"What happened?" asked Susan walking up to her boss. "Did he threaten you?"

"Ty's dead," he remarked flatly.

"Excuse me? He's dead?" asked the astonished chef.

"Yea, he's kind of a blue color. Like he couldn't breathe or something," said Jay still pacing. "It looks like he was eating some of the clam chowder."

Boyd came crashing through the swinging kitchen doors.

"Sorry," he said looking at the door. "What's going on?"

"My first executive chef, Ty Fenster, is dead in the office," answered Jay solemnly.

"Dead? I had better call Ed. We don't need the paramedics," said Boyd, walking towards the office.

"Has anyone been in there?" he asked, looking through the door.

"Only me," said Jay. "I didn't touch anything except to feel for a pulse on the side of his neck. I saw Ty was dead and then came back out."

"You finding dead bodies is starting to become common place," said the Chief, pulling out his radio. "Dispatch, this is Boyd. Can you send the coroner to The Shipwreck Café?"

"Who was the last one to talk to him when he was alive?"

"I guess that would be me," answered Susan, stepping forward.

"And you are?" asked Boyd, taking out a notebook.

"Susan Myers, second executive chef."

"Second, huh?"

"What's that supposed to mean?" demanded Susan.

"Nothing, nothing at all. When was the last time you talked to him?"

"About two hours ago. He grabbed some food and said he would be in the office ordering tomorrow's produce," she answered.

"You didn't talk to him after that?" asked Boyd, scribbling in his little book.

"I was too busy doing his job and mine," she replied angrily.

"I take it you didn't like Mr. Fenster?"

"No, I didn't, and neither did anyone else around this kitchen," she answered sharply.

"You didn't see anyone else go in or out of the office?"

"I told you, I was too busy. Are we done here?" she asked, crossing her arms.

"Yea, but don't leave Anchor Point," the Chief responded,

closing his notebook.

"I'll see you in the morning, boss," said Susan. "Can I have my purse? It's on the bottom shelf of the bookcase."

"I need to check that before you leave," said Boyd, reaching for the purse.

"Seriously?" she replied handing it over to him.

He rummaged through the contents. Keys, make-up, a wallet, assorted snacks, and protein bars were contained in the purse. Nothing caught his eye, so he gave it back to Susan.

"Okay, you can go," he said, turning his attention back to the dead body.

Susan left in a huff. Josh came back to the kitchen with the coroner and his assistant. No one caught the fact that the sous chef had slipped out without saying anything to anyone.

"Jay, we meet again."

"Not funny, Ed," Jay responded, watching the Chief poking around the office.

"So, where's the body?"

"In the office. Stephen's already there," answered Jay pointing the way.

The coroner entered the office and went directly over to the dead man. He walked around the body examining it from all directions. Next, he opened the mouth and looked in with a flashlight.

"The throat is swollen closed. From the blue tint to his skin, I would say this man died from lack of oxygen due to allergic reaction. Is that what he was eating?" he asked, pointing to the bowl of chowder.

"The spoon is on the floor so I guess we would assume so. Don't you think?"

"It doesn't make sense. If he had a severe shellfish allergy, why would he be eating chowder?" asked Ed. "Did he list an allergy on his application?"

"If he did, I didn't notice," answered Jay. "It's not a regular question that we ask. I can check to see if he listed it on his insurance information. I'll be right back."

"Chief, can you make sure you bag the chowder and spoon and send it to my lab?" Ed requested. "While you're at it, you might as well bag the water bottle, too."

Jay returned and handed the application packet to Boyd.

"He's not allergic to seafood. But, he did list a severe allergy to peanuts," said Jay. "It's on his insurance form as a pre-existing medical condition."

"Does your Mom's recipe have any peanuts or peanut based products in it?" Boyd inquired.

"No, it doesn't," Jay responded.

"We'll need to take the batch of chowder that this came bowl came from. Is that possible?" asked the coroner.

"We only had one container of chowder left at the end of the night. I'll get it from the walk-in," Jay offered.

Jay retrieved the plastic bucket of chowder and set it on the table next to the kitchen door. Standing just outside the office door, he watched the process of collecting evidence. It never failed to amaze him how even the smallest thing could be used to determine a cause of death.

A cold patch of air materialized next to his right arm. Words were whispered in his ear.

"Where is the pocket watch?"

Jay stepped into the office and walked over to the body and checked it closely.

"Are you looking for something in particular?" asked Ed.

"Ty checked a pocket watch the last time I saw him in the kitchen. From where I was standing, it looked to be expensive and made of gold. I was wondering where it was," answered Jay. "It's not in his pocket."

"Check the desk drawers," suggested Boyd. "I'll look around over here."

The room was searched, but no pocket watch was found.

Robbie came into the kitchen with a clipboard in his hands.

"Dude, what is going on?" he asked his brother.

"Robbie, where have you been the last two hours?" Boyd questioned.

"Is that TY?" Robbie asked in horror.

"Robbie, where have you been?" asked Boyd again.

"I've been down cellar doing inventory on the liquor and wine. We sold a lot tonight and I needed to do an order for the morning," Robbie answered. "I've been down there since the restaurant closed. Peter was covering the bar upstairs. Why?"

"Suspicious death," was all Boyd would say.

"I didn't even know the dude," said Robbie. "I said "hi" to him earlier when he came up to the bar, which I thought was kind of strange him being in uniform and all."

"He was upstairs?" asked Jay, frowning. "What the hell was he doing up there?"

"I don't know. He poked around the bar area, grabbed a bottle of sherry, and left," Robbie responded.

"I don't see any sherry bottle anywhere in the office. I wonder what he did with it," said the Chief, thinking out loud.

"It's down cellar," answered Robbie. "I saw it on a shelf downstairs. He didn't even use it."

"That's weird," Ed commented. "Why did he take it in the first place?"

"I don't know, but things aren't adding up here," said Boyd.

"Ed, are you ready to take the body?"

"Yea, we'll be out of here in five minutes."

"Jay, don't let anyone in here until I tell you it's okay. Your chef will be a little late tomorrow. I saw peanuts and peanut butter protein bars in her purse. Maybe, she didn't like being second in charge after all."

"Susan doesn't appear to be that kind of person," said Jay, shaking his head. "I don't think she had anything to do with this."

The body was packed up and rolled away. The Chief started to hang crime scene tape across the office door.

"Can I put the computer on standby before you close off the office?" asked Jay.

"Sure," said Boyd watching him to make sure he did nothing else while in the room.

"Have you found anything on Bea's killer yet?" Jay inquired as they walked to the front door.

"No, no one saw anything. There's so many fingerprints in the building it's hard to sort through them, and so far, the only things we know are missing are the maps to this place and the safe contents."

"Have you found out what was in the safe?" asked Jay, unlocking the front door.

"It seems only Bea knew the contents."

"There was someone else who knew what was in there. Obviously, the murderer did. He made her open the safe and took the contents," Jay thought out loud.

"True," Boyd answered. "But, how did he know?"

"That's what we need to figure out," Jay observed.

"We?" asked the Chief.

Jay ignored the last question posed to him. These events were going to affect his business and his life; you could be real sure he was going to be looking for answers. People were going to question the safety of his mother's chowder recipe. This could definitely hurt his new business if those answers weren't found, and found quickly.

"Ed, please let me know when you find out anything," asked Jay as the coroner climbed into the wagon.

"This is a bummer. What a crappy ending to a great day," Robbie commented, walking up behind him. "Do you need me for anything else? I'm beat, I hear my bed calling me."

"No, I'm good. Thanks for today. You did an awesome job, Robbie."

"Peter and I did almost three-hundred each in tips tonight. I know it won't be this busy all the time, but I'll take it while I can."

"I won't be far behind you. I'm going to empty the register and shut down the computers. Do me a favor and let Stormy out of the office for me. She needs to run around for a while."

"Sure. See you tomorrow."

Jay ran the daily reports and shut down the system. He was loading the money into a deposit bag when Stormy came racing across the waiting area. Her tail was wagging faster than her butt could keep up with. He laughed as he hugged his dog, and Stormy covered him with kisses. The staff had visited her in the office all day long so she wasn't alone for any great length of time. Jay was sure she was going to become spoiled very quickly.

"Come on, girl. Let's shut out the lights and go home," Jay blew out a heavy sigh.

He picked up the bag of money as Stormy looked upwards growling. The ghost was standing at the top of the stairs.

"Good night, Roland. Everyone's gone. It will be quiet until my Mom and Mary get here early in the morning."

The ghost nodded once and disappeared.

Chapter 9

JAY WAS LYING in bed when he suddenly remembered that neither Mary or his mother knew what had happened last night. Since it was a few minutes before seven, they were probably already at the café.

"Come on, girl. We need to hurry," said Jay, throwing on a pair of jeans and a tee shirt.

Stormy stopped at her bowl waiting to be fed.

"No time right now. I'll feed you something when we get back," Jay stated opening the door.

On the way to the café, Stormy stopped at every bush she came upon. Jay couldn't leave her outside by herself so he had to patiently wait for her to do her business. He entered through the front door so the dog would not be in the kitchen. Cracking the kitchen door open, he asked Mary and his mother to come out.

Martha came out of the kitchen with a deep frown on her face. Mary followed behind, head down.

"Jay, why is there police tape across the office door?" his mother asked.

"I don't like to be near where dead people are found," Mary said quietly.

"I wanted to get here before you did this morning to warn you. Ty died in the office late last night and the Chief says it's another murder. It seems Ty had a severe peanut allergy and someone fed him peanuts without him knowing."

"How would he not know?" Martha questioned.

"Ed seems to think it was in the clam chowder. You don't

put any peanut products in your chowder, do you, Mom?" asked Jay.

"No, none at all," she insisted.

"That's exactly what I told the Chief," her son replied. "Mary, are you okay?"

"Yes, sir," she answered, looking at the floor.

"The office door is locked and no one else is here. Can you go back and start the chowder while I talk to my Mom, please?"

"I suppose," she said, shrugging her shoulders and shuffling away.

"She is one strange girl," Martha whispered.

Jay waited until Mary had gone through the swinging doors before he spoke. He explained what had happened the night before and what was said. He told her that the Chief was suspicious of Susan because of the food she had in her purse. Martha was visibly upset that they thought Susan had something to do with it.

He asked his mother to keep a look-out for anyone that had a gold pocket watch since Ty's had been stolen off the dead body and was unaccounted for. He told her to be careful, to not go anywhere by herself, and to trust only him and Robbie.

"Roland told me he didn't trust Ty. Now, it looks like there is someone else who can be trusted even less," said his Mom. "For a dead man, he sure knows how to judge people."

"Mom, you were good friends with Bea, right?" asked Jay.

"If you call sitting with her once a week at bingo being friends, I guess so. Not good friends, but friends," she answered.

"Why?"

"The volunteers at the historical society said Bea was the only one who knew the contents of the safe in the back room. But, the person who killed her must have known what was in there. He made her open the safe and took the contents along with three maps to this property."

"You think it has something to do with the treasure, don't

you?" she asked.

"Yes, I do. I believe Ty was somehow involved in what is happening around here. I need to find out what was in that safe and why it was so important," Jay declared.

"I can think of only one other person who might know what was in there," said Martha. "But, he doesn't live here anymore."

"Who is it?"

"Do you remember Mr. Peterson?"

"The guy who owned the penny-candy store at the edge of town?" Jay recalled.

"Yes. Bea would never marry him, but they did date for many years. He spent a lot of time at the historical society with her. If anyone knows, he would," Martha suggested.

"Where is he?"

"His kids put him in an assisted living facility up in Plymouth. Cottonwood, I think," she answered. "I believe he's still alive."

"You're the best. Keep our conversations on the mum, okay? Don't even discuss them with Mary while you are cooking," said Jay, hugging her. "By the way, the Chief took the extra bucket of chowder to test it for peanuts. So, you are starting out at zero for lunch. You might need to make an extra batch so we have enough for tonight. Be careful, Mom."

Jay called Cindy to see if she wanted to take a ride on Friday. It was his only day off and he needed to go talk to Mr. Peterson, but she was working and couldn't go. He decided to ask his Mom if she wanted to go instead. It might prove helpful having someone there that he would remember from the past.

Jay and Stormy exited by the front door and returned to the cottage to have breakfast. The truck that filled the mechanical newspaper dispenser was just pulling away. Jay decided to grab a paper since his café story was supposed to run on the front page. He looked through the window of the dispenser as he deposited the coins in the slot. He felt sick.

In the center of the front page, was the picture of Jay cutting the red ribbon. Standing behind him was his Mom, his brother, and just inside the door was the faint outline of Roland. Jay held the paper closer. Yes, it was the ghost. You could see right through him to the plant sitting on the half wall at the hostess station.

How could Gabe not see this? Why didn't he call me before he printed this on the front page?

"Come on, girl. I have some phone calls to make," Jay stated in irritation.

Before he called Gabe at the paper, he scanned the accompanying article. In it, the reporter gave a small history of the lighthouse. Included in that history was the fact that the lighthouse was reported to be haunted and a buried treasure from a hundred years ago, belonging to Roland Knowles, said ghost, could or could not be still hidden on the property.

The reporter had captured a picture of the ghost which would give the missing treasure story some validation. People would be swarming all over the property. This is exactly what Bea had warned him about; money makes people crazy. Jay didn't need this extra aggravation on top of the murder that already had taken place here tied to the treasure story.

"This is not good, Stormy," said Jay, dialing his cell.

Jay ended up talking to Gabe for twenty minutes. The reporter told him it was the only picture the ghost had been in. He thought it would be good for café's business if people thought they could have supper and see a ghost at the same time. He apologized when he realized how mad Jay was.

"Damage has been done," Jay grumbled. "I just hope things don't get crazy around here with treasure hunters destroying my property."

"I'm really sorry, Jay. You're not going to sue the paper, are you?" asked Gabe. "I mean, you being an attorney and all?"

"We'll see what happens," said Jay, purposely not giving a

firm answer. "I have to go."

The chaos started Sunday afternoon. Television trucks, reporters from off Cape, and every person who wanted to get rich quick were wandering around the property. Jay even found one guy inside his cottage rifling through his private things looking for a clue to the treasure. The intruder had locked poor Stormy in the bathroom. Jay called the police and had him arrested.

In front of all the television cameras, Chief Boyd made the announcement that this was private property and anyone caught trespassing would be arrested and thrown in jail. He made his point by putting the man who had broken into Jay's private residence into the cruiser, handcuffed. He turned to say one more thing before he left for the station.

"I have lived here all my life. I know all the stories of Roland Knowles' buried treasure. I'm sure somewhere in the last one hundred years the treasure was found and taken away. Maybe Roland's ghost is here, but I'm real sure the treasure is not."

Over the next couple of days, the crowds died out as the reporters moved on to other more important stories. The police had made nine arrests in three days. The thrill of the hunt was squashed by the fact that the police were watching over the property.

People came for dinner hoping to get a glimpse of the ghost, but he was never seen in public. Martha had warned him to stay clear of the café, telling him his picture had been taken and put in the newspapers. Roland was content to wander around at night when the place was empty. He only made himself visible to Martha and Jay.

Roland's favorite place to hang out early in the morning and late at night, was the bar. It amused the ghost that Robbie couldn't see him and was afraid of him. The younger brother would freak out when the ghost slid a glass down the bar or the napkins would fly in the air after Robbie had just finished stacking them. The ghost's favorite thing to do was to take Robbie's ordering clipboard and hide it on him. Roland would never hurt him because of his promise to the boy's Mom; but, he did enjoy annoying him.

When the restaurant opened, Roland would disappear up to the lighthouse for peace and quiet. Jay made the decision to scrap the private dining for special occasions in the lighthouse. He couldn't bring himself to take away the only place the ghost had to himself.

As a peace offering to the ghost for losing his freedom of wandering the place day and night, Jay roped off the small section where Bea's table had been and placed a new, high powered telescope there for Roland's enjoyment. It looked out over the point so that the lighthouse keeper could continue to watch for ships even in his after-life.

The coroner called Jay on Wednesday morning to tell him the container of chowder from the walk-in was clean. The only place they found peanut residue was in the half-eaten bowl in the office.

This meant someone specifically targeted Ty Fenster. Jay wished he had the cameras in the kitchen installed before the café had opened. The only working cameras were at the front door and on the register. The kitchen and the loading dock area were to be installed in the second phase. Whoever killed Ty knew the cameras in the kitchen weren't recording yet. They had to have come in the back door or already been at work. If they were in uniform, no one would have given them a second look. There was a killer walking amongst them.

The next few days passed without incident. Business was steady, but nothing like it had been the first day. The summer tourists were more predominant on the weekends. Once school was out, the café would be filled with unfamiliar faces all week long.

Robbie was in charge while Jay was not on the premises. Jay stopped at the café to tell his brother that he and their Mom were heading off Cape. He checked on Mary to make sure she was okay with making the chowder herself. She said she had watched Martha enough times that she was comfortable handling it on her own.

As he drove down the hill, he saw Roland standing on the lighthouse catwalk in his side mirror. Jay figured with him and his Mom not there for the ghost to visit, he would torment Robbie all morning instead. It was going to be a long morning for his brother.

Martha was standing in the front yard waiting for her son. They stopped at The Burger Box, grabbed two coffees and two apple spice muffins to go. Stormy sat in the back seat with her nose out the window while they drove.

"Let me talk to George first," suggested his Mom. "He hasn't seen you in a long time."

"Good idea," agreed Jay.

"And, I don't want him to know what happened to Bea. I am going to tell him she passed away and nothing more. He doesn't need to know the gory details of her death."

"I don't want Mr. Peterson upset. I just want to know if he knows the contents of the safe," Jay responded.

They pulled into the parking lot of The Cottonwood Assisted Living Facility. Jay had called the staff to let them know that he and his Mom were coming to visit Mr. Peterson. He was sitting in the lobby waiting for them when they walked through the doors; his face lit up when he saw Martha.

They checked in at the receptionist's desk and walked over to greet George. He was in a wheelchair, unable to stand on his own. Martha leaned in and gave her old friend a bear hug. He had tears in his eyes, he was so happy to see her.

"Martha, you look wonderful," said George as she sat on the couch next to him. "How long has it been?"

"At least four years," she answered. "How are you doing?"

"You know, getting old. But it's nice here. I do miss my friends in Anchor Point," he said, sighing. "How are you doing? Still at the gossip parlor?"

"No. Theresa and I were moving to Florida, but her daughter has cancer so she's staying here to help with the kids. Speaking of kids, do you remember my oldest son, Jeremy?"

"Jay, right," he asked, reaching to shake hands.

"Yes, sir," he replied with a smile. "That's what you used to call me in your store."

"So, what do I owe this visit to?" asked George. "I'm sure you didn't come by to just visit me?"

"We need your help, my friend," started Martha, taking his hand.

"How can I help you in here?"

"I have some bad news for you. Bea passed on last week," said Martha, closely watching for an adverse reaction from him.

"Bea's gone?" he repeated, tearing up. "What happened?"

"We're trying to find out. That's why we need your help."

"Anything to help my sweet Bea," said George, wiping away a tear that was sliding down his cheek. "I tried for fifteen years to get that gal to marry me and she just wouldn't. I never did understand why."

"Even though she didn't, I know she loved you with every inch of her being, my friend," said Martha, smiling at him.

"How can I help you? Anything…"

"Do you remember when you used to spend time at The Historical Society with Bea?"

"Sure, we spent many hours at her work. I read so many books and learned something new every day," he answered.

"Do you remember a small safe that was kept in the backroom?" asked Jay.

"That was Bea's private safe. She kept it there instead of her house because the building was alarmed and her house wasn't," explained George. "Why do you ask?"

"The building was broken into and the contents of the safe were stolen along with three maps. No one knows what was inside the safe. The police are hoping if they could learn what was taken, it might lead them to the suspect," Jay explained.

"If the contents were gone, then Bea had to be the one to open the safe. No one else knew the combination, not even me," said George.

"Do you know what was in the safe?" asked Jay again.

"Wait a minute. If Bea opened the safe during the robbery… is that how she died? Did someone murder my Bea?" he asked, staring at Martha.

"Yes, George. She was murdered for the contents of that safe. Now do you see why it is so important that we find out what was in there?" asked Martha.

"This is really strange," he said, drifting off in thought.

"What, George? What is strange?" asked Martha, trying to bring him back to the present.

"A young man came to visit me about a month back. He was asking the same questions you are asking now. He wanted to know what was in the safe. At the time, I thought it strange, but he said he was related to Bea and was looking for information on their family history," answered the old man.

"What did you tell him?" asked Jay.

"I told him it wasn't my place to give out personal information on someone else."

"Was he mad that you wouldn't tell him anything?" asked Martha.

"More like furious. I told him if he was related to Bea to go talk to her about the family history. Oh dear, I sent him right to Bea, didn't I?" he replied in horror.

"You didn't know. And he would have found his way there eventually, my friend," said Martha, consoling him. "You did nothing wrong."

"He wasn't related to Bea, was he? He wanted to know what was in the safe," George realized.

"George, do you know what was in the safe and why it was so important?" Martha repeated.

"Yes, I do. Bea had all her family's legal papers in there. Her will, insurance policies, and family birth certificates were kept in that safe. But there is something more important that I am sure the thief wanted," George confided. "I had forgotten all about it until now."

"Forgotten about what, George?"

"Bea came from the Knowles bloodline. Forty some years ago, her great uncle, I can't remember his name, died and left everything to Bea. One of the boxes she opened after his funeral contained a gold pocket watch and hand-written diary of Roland Knowles. I was the only other person who knew she had inherited those items."

"Someone else knew, George, and figured out where Bea kept them," Jay responded. "I'll be right back."

Jay left the two old friends talking while he went to the front desk. He checked the sign in book for signatures of people who had visited and who they had visited. Thirty-six days prior to their visit, George's name showed up in the log as being called on. The sign in signature of the person visiting also read George Peterson; whoever it was had covered their tracks.

"Excuse me," Jay interrupted, smiling his best smile at the receptionist. "I see you have cameras around the facility. Are they in working order?"

"Yes, they are. They run twenty-four hours, seven days a week," she answered.

"So, if someone visited, say thirty-six days ago, it would be on film?"

"No. The tapes are kept on a rotating basis and reused after thirty days. Those days would have been taped over already. Why? Is there a problem?"

"Mr. Peterson was visited at that time by a man who we are trying to identify. I was hoping you had his image on tape," explained Jay.

"I remember that guy. The only reason I do is poor Mr. Peterson was so upset when he left that we had to sedate him to calm him down," the receptionist recalled.

"Can you describe him to me?"

"Sure. About thirty to thirty-five years old, big build, dark hair, and a bad temper. Twice I had to tell him to keep his voice down. The third time, I finally asked him to leave."

"Did he leave quietly?" Jay inquired.

"Not really. He pushed over a tray stand on his way out. It's funny though, he

came in the door in a cook's uniform and I thought he was here for work. He got real indignant when I asked him if he was here to see the head chef for a job. He informed me in a nasty tone of voice that he would never work in a dump like this, and soon he wouldn't have to work at all."

"Thanks so much. You have been really helpful," Jay complimented.

He turned away to watch his Mom with her friend. She must have changed the subject because the two of them were laughing and smiling together. The receptionist came around the counter and stood next to Jay.

"Now, that's the way we like to see our visits go," she said, smiling up at him.

"Thanks, again," Jay replied, walking away.

"Mom. I'm going outside to let Stormy out for a walk. You visit with George and I'll be back in a bit," Jay stated.

The dog was sitting up in the back seat watching everything around her. Her whole body wiggled in happiness when she saw Jay coming across the parking lot. He put on her leash, grabbed a roll of poop bags out of the glove compartment, and set off for a walk.

He called Boyd to let him know what they had found out from George; Jay was pretty sure the visitor had been Ty. He also told the police Chief what the contents of the safe had been. Jay told Boyd he believed the gold pocket watch he had seen Ty with the day he was murdered must have come from the safe. Jay also told Boyd that he thought the gold chain in the dead woman's hand must have come from the pocket watch. He believed the chef was the one who killed Bea Thomas, but there was still no way to prove it.

Their walk lasted over an hour. This gave his Mom and George plenty of time to reminisce about the old days. Jay and Stormy stood outside the door waiting for Martha to come out. The dog spotted her first and the tail started swishing at top speed. George must have made a comment about the dog, because Martha wheeled his chair over to the door so he could see her.

As the door automatically opened, the dog pulled the leash right out of Jay's hand, bounding forward for who they thought would be Martha. But, instead Stormy jumped up on George, licking his face and going crazy. She tried to crawl up in his lap, but the wheelchair didn't provide room for the dog to get up there.

"She looks just like my Angie," George commented, smiling. "And acts like her, too. How old is she?"

"I don't truthfully know, sir. She was abandoned and living at the lighthouse when I bought the place. I took her in about two months ago," explained Jay.

"At the lighthouse, you say?"

"Yes, sir. Why?"

"Why? Because I'm spitting mad right now. Damn kids of mine. They put me in here six months ago but I couldn't bring my Angie with me. They don't allow animals here. Robin promised me they would find a good home for my dog. Instead, they obviously abandoned her and she returned to the last place we were together, looking for me."

"Are you sure this is Angie?" asked Jay, doubting the old man's memory.

"Watch," he ordered.

"Angie, sit," he commanded.

The dog sat immediately.

George raised his pointer finger straight up in the air. The dog sat up on her hind quarters. To prove it even further, the old man made the same finger go in a circle. The golden grabbed her tail in her mouth and spun in circles as George kept his finger moving. The finger stopped, the dog stopped. She sat patiently waiting for the next command.

"Yup, this is my Angie," he said, hugging the dog in delight.

"Mr. Peterson, I don't want you to worry about her. She has a good home and is spoiled rotten. Everyone loves her at the restaurant. She's kind of the café's mascot. We live in the caretaker's cottage and she loves to run the beach," said Jay, trying to ease the old man's suffering at finding out she had been abandoned.

"You promise you'll take good care of her? She's real special, you know. Angie is one of the smartest dogs I ever had," he said, not letting go off his now found pet.

"I guess now that we know her real name we'll have to call her Angie," said Jay. "If you like, I will bring Angie to visit you once a month. Right now, I can't promise any more than that as I just opened a new restaurant in the lighthouse and summer is upon us. You know from owning the candy store how busy the Cape is during tourist season."

"You opened a restaurant at the lighthouse? Have you seen him? Angie doesn't like him at all," George questioned.

"Are you talking about the ghost?" asked Martha.

"Yup. I don't know why, but Angie growled at him every time he was near us," confided the old man. "Didn't you, girl?"

"She still does," Jay replied with a grin.

"You promise me you'll bring her to visit?" asked George with a gleam in his eye.

"We promise," she assured him. "Maybe, in the Fall we can kidnap you and bring you down to the café for supper. Would you like that?"

"I would love to see Anchor Point again. I'm just so relieved to know where my Angie is and that she's happy," he said hugging the dog and crying. "Thank you, Jay. You'll never know how much this means to me."

"I think I love her just as much as you do, sir," Jay responded smiling.

"I can tell you do, son," he said letting the dog go. "Martha, get me back inside so I can call those no-good kids of mine and tell them what I think of them. Jay, I'll be looking forward to those visits and if I can help in any other way, just call me."

He reached out to shake Jay's hand and then gave the dog one final kiss on the head. Martha returned him to the lobby where she hugged and kissed him and promised to see him soon.

Mother and son returned to Anchor Point. He dropped her off at the beauty parlor so she could see her friends and catch up on the local town gossip.

Jay and Stormy, now Angie, returned to the cottage together. It was going to take Jay some time to get used to calling the dog by her new, old name. The golden didn't seem to care and answered to both.

He grabbed a beer and they sat on the back deck of the cottage. Angie stretched out next to Jay, soaking in the warm sun. This was the life Jay wanted. This was why he returned to the Cape. He closed his eyes, drank his beer, and worked on his tan. His arm fell over the side of the chair landing on his dog's warm fur. He stoked her lovingly while they sat listening to the crashing waves in the distance and enjoying their day off on Cape Cod.

Chapter 10

BUSINESS BECAME MORE steady as June passed and Fourth of July Weekend approached. The café was busy now from open to close. The yellow tape had finally been removed from the office door and Susan had been cleared of any wrongdoing. It was on record at the local health food store that she had been ordering those snacks and protein bars for over a year before the murder. She was now the first executive chef in charge of the kitchen and under her direction, the kitchen ran smoothly and everyone was happy to be at work.

Thoughts of buried treasure and dead bodies had been left behind in the hustle and bustle of the busy tourist season. It had never left Jay's mind that there still could be a killer working in his kitchen. During his walk-throughs of the cafe, he was constantly looking for that gold watch or anything that seemed strange or out of place. Martha also kept an eye on everyone in the kitchen. Nothing happened that she didn't know or hear about.

Jay was in his office opening the café mail and Angie was curled up on her bed next to the desk. An envelope with a return address of Cottonwood Assisted Living Facility caught his eye. He pulled it out of the pile and opened it; several letters inside the facility envelope fell out.

A short note from the director of Cottonwood explained that Mr. Peterson had passed away. The enclosed letters were to be mailed directly to Jay and not given to his children per his request. He had told one of the nurses on his floor that he was ready to go be with Bea, his long-time love. Knowing that his dog had a good home, he didn't have to worry about her anymore either. He felt free to meet Bea on the other side and he passed in his sleep that very night.

Jay opened the letter from George first, noticing that the handwriting was barely legible.

Dear Mr. Hallett,

If you are reading this letter I have moved on. I am with my sweet Bea and we are finally happy.

Several days after your visit, I received a letter in the mail from Bea's attorney. She had written me a letter to be delivered upon her death. After all these years, I finally received the answer as to why she would not marry me; she was already married to someone else. Many years before we met, her Father had promised her to another man, Redmond Jules. He was apparently a man of wealth and reputation. They married, even though Bea had told her Father she didn't love him and that she loved someone else. Bea's family had strong Amish roots and women did as they were told.

Over the next three years Bea had two children, Emily and Redmond. It was later discovered the children were not her husband's, but were fathered by the man she loved and had been seeing secretly while she had been married. The children were taken away and sent to an orphanage, and Bea was beaten to within an inch of her life.

Not knowing where her children were or if they were even still alive, Bea left in the middle of the night with only the clothes on her back, some personal papers, and enough money to pay for a train ticket. She ended up in Boston.

Not wanting to be found by her husband, she changed her last name to Thomas. She moved to the Cape, under the pretense of being a young widow and no one had ever questioned her. She lived there happily from that point on.

Over the years, she searched for her children. The only

thing she did find out was that her daughter had two children. They were taken by the state when Emily had been murdered in a robbery attempt. No names or locations were recorded on paper. She never found her son or anything about him. She had given up on finding them right before she met me.

Bea took the job at the historical society and learned through research that she was related to Roland Knowles. Bea's mother's maiden name was Fenster. Roland Knowles was her great, great uncle on her mother's side.

When the historical society moved to the building it's located in now, Bea was given the job of sorting and categorizing years and years of boxes of items that had been donated to the society. In one of these boxes she found the original diary and gold pocket watch of Roland Knowles. There was no mention of who had donated the box. Bea decided that because she was a descendant it would help her research her family history. She kept the two items for herself, not telling anyone she took them. From that day forward, they stayed in her private safe in the back room along with her and her children's birth certificates. All these years, she lied to me about inheriting the two pieces.

In the diary, Roland refers to the treasure buried on the property. Several clues were given throughout the entries. Over the years, while the lighthouse was abandoned, Bea would walk the property looking for the treasure. She never found it.

I am enclosing her letter, copies of all the paperwork her attorney sent to me, and a copy of my last will and testament.

My attorney will be in touch with you. I have made you trustee of my estate. My children have been excluded from the will because of what they did to Angie. I am leaving my money in a trust for you to disburse to animal shelters and animal hospitals that need financial help. It is a goodly sum and my children will probably fight the new will. Stick to your guns for the animals' sakes. My attorney has been instructed to do the same.

Tell Martha I treasured her friendship. Jay, I hold you in the highest esteem for what you did for my Angie. Have a wonderful life and please say hi to the ghost for me.

Your friend,
George Peterson

Jay sat back in his chair and heaved a heavy sigh. How was this information going to help him? He knew that Ty had the gold pocket watch which put him at the scene of Bea's murder. He had used the last name of Fenster on his application. What was his real name?

The first thing Jay had to do was tell his mother of her friend's death. Sighing, he got up from his chair; Angie lifted her head, but decided she wasn't done napping. Jay reached down to pat her on the head.

"Your master just made a lot of your friends very happy," Jay confided to her, thinking about the donations to the shelters. "People, not so much."

His Mom wasn't in the kitchen. Mary was stirring the two big kettles of chowder alone. He walked to the stove and grabbed a clean coffee mug and dipped it into the closest kettle. Mary stared at him in consternation.

"Quality control," Jay offered up, chuckling.

Mary didn't get the joke and if she did, she didn't even crack a smile.

"Never mind. Have you seen my Mom?" he asked.

"Last I know she was taking a batch of chowder to the walk-in," said Mary. "If you find her, please tell her I have to leave in ten minutes and the chowder won't be done before then. I don't want it to catch on and burn."

Susan was in the office entering the day's orders. Everyone else was hustling around the kitchen getting ready for the opening rush in just thirty minutes. Jay entered the walk-in and saw his mother lying in a crumpled heap in the far corner. Chowder covered the entire floor around her.

He leaned out of the walk-in and yelled desperately for help; Susan was the first one to respond to his call. Together, they carried his mother out to the warmth of the kitchen but she wasn't responding. Jay pulled out his cell and called nine-one-one.

"Mom, wake up. Can you hear me?" he asked, rubbing her hands to warm them up. "Susan, go get Robbie."

The kitchen staff gathered quickly around the scene; several asked what they could do to help. The others just stood there staring. Jay could almost read their minds as he looked at the scared faces around him. One dead chef and now Martha was found in the walk-in not responding. How could he assure them that they were safe at their jobs? He knew he couldn't.

Robbie stormed into the kitchen and knelt at his Mom's side.

"Jay, what happened?"

"I don't know. I found her in the walk-in covered in chowder," Jay responded, picking up her head and cradling it in his lap.

He looked down at his hands and saw they were covered with blood. Jay tilted her head and could see a huge gash was bleeding profusely at the back of her head.

"Susan, I need clean towels," Jay yelled out.

The ambulance sirens could be heard screaming in the distance as Chief Boyd rushed into the kitchen.

"I heard on the dispatch," he said. "Oh, jeez, not Martha now. What happened?"

"I haven't been able to check the walk-in. I don't know if she was attacked or if she slid on something and hit her head. Can you check? Far corner, to the right," Jay instructed.

"I'll be right back," the Chief acknowledged.

Susan told the staff to get back to work as the café opened in

DEATH BY CHOWDAH

ten minutes' time and they had to be ready. She kept everyone busy and focused on what needed to be done.

The paramedics arrived and they took Martha's vitals and put a temporary wrap on her head to help slow down the bleeding. She was lifted onto the gurney to be transported to Anchor Point General Hospital.

"Robbie, go with Mom. I'll meet you at the hospital," Jay insisted.

Jay entered the walk-in looking for the Chief and saw he was frowning.

"Do you have a large plastic bag?" he asked Jay. "Don't touch anything."

Jay returned with a large plastic bag and rubber gloves. The Chief had already put on latex gloves. He reached underneath one of the shelves and brought out a bloody rolling pin which he held up for Jay to see.

"I don't think your mother slipped and fell," said Boyd.

Jay was angry; no, he was furious now.

"How am I supposed to protect the people who work here?" he asked the Chief in frustration.

"I don't know what to tell you, Jay. Have you got the cameras hooked up back here yet?"

"Coast Alarms is supposed to be here Monday to hook them up," Jay replied. "I've even requested that extra cameras be installed so that every corner of the kitchen and stock area will be covered."

Boyd looked around the kitchen; the café had opened for lunch and the staff was busy filling food orders. No one had any interest in what was happening in the walk-in. Mary Chase walked up to her boss, head down.

"Mr. Hallett, I was supposed to go home an hour ago. Can I put the chowder away and leave now?" she asked, just one notch over a whisper.

"Sorry, Mary. Yes, can you put the chowder in the back

walk-in? I need to get maintenance to clean up the front one. Thanks for staying. Before you go, did you see anyone near the walk-in besides my mother?" Jay quizzed.

"No, Mr. Hallett. I was stirring the chowder," Mary answered solemnly.

"I know tomorrow is your day off, but I don't think my Mom will be coming into work. Is there any way you can take her shift? I'll put an extra bonus in your check," he offered as compensation.

"I guess so," she shrugged. "I'll be here at seven."

"I appreciate it. Thank you," said Jay as she walked away.

"Whatever…" she mumbled.

"Is she all there?" the Chief asked Jay.

"Sometimes I wonder," Jay answered honestly.

"I'm going to get this to the lab and see if they can lift any fingerprints," said Boyd holding up the plastic bag. "I'll call you with any results."

"I have some interesting things to tell you, but I need to get to the hospital to check on my Mom," said Jay. "Can you swing by tomorrow sometime to talk?"

"I'll be here at eleven," he answered, heading for the door.

"Susan, you're in charge with me and Robbie gone. I'll be at the hospital. Call me if you have any problems. You have my cell number, right?"

"Yes, I do. Jay, I hope Martha is all right. I so adore that woman," she offered, concerned.

"I'll be back as soon as I can," Jay replied.

As soon as Jay entered the emergency room entrance, he saw Robbie and Theresa waiting in the lobby.

"What have you heard?" asked Jay.

"Nothing. Mom's still unconscious. She's down in x-ray right now," Robbie filled him in. "The Doc says she got hit pretty hard."

"I know. We found the rolling pin after you left," Jay

shared.

"Seriously? Who would do something like that to your mother?" asked Theresa in astonishment.

"I don't know. Maybe, she saw something she wasn't supposed to see," Jay answered as he gave Theresa a hug.

"This probably sounds crazy, but do you think Roland saw anything?" asked Robbie.

Before Jay could answer, Cindy came rushing through the doors of the lobby. It looked like half the town was following close behind. They crowded around the brothers asking questions. Robbie tried to get the locals to sit down but there weren't enough seats to accommodate everyone who was there to find out about Martha.

"We don't know anything yet," announced Jay. "Mom is still in x-ray being checked out. I appreciate all of you coming down here to check on her, but we may not know anything for quite a while yet."

A wave of murmurs rolled over the lobby. People were trying to decide whether to stay or go.

"We'll wait," said Lorna Grund, owner of the local beauty parlor and Martha's ex-boss.

Everyone else nodded in agreement. Magazines and newspapers were grabbed in anticipation of the long wait. Theresa told Jay she would be back later because she had to go home and check on her daughter who had just gotten home from the hospital herself after completing her first chemo treatment. Jay, Robbie, and Cindy moved to the vending machine room to have a private conversation.

"I don't know if we can stay open with everything that's happening," Robbie worried, shaking his head. "I mean, I know it's your business, Jay, but people are getting hurt."

"What do you mean?" asked Cindy. "This wasn't an accident?"

"No, it wasn't. Someone clobbered my Mom with a rolling

pin," answered Jay. "Robbie, you are thinking exactly what the suspect is wanting us to think."

"What do you mean?"

"I think whoever is doing this wants the café shut down. Wouldn't it be easier to search for the treasure if no one was around?" reasoned Jay.

"Are you saying this all goes back to the Knowles' treasure?" Cindy asked, wide eyed.

"Yes, I am. Mom and I found out what was in the safe that Bea died for. It was a gold pocket watch and a journal belonging to Roland Knowles. The journal contains clues to where the treasure is buried," he explained. "Bea searched for it for years but never found it."

"So, whoever is responsible for the events at the café found out what was in the safe and killed to get it," said Cindy.

"But, how did they find out? George Peterson was the only other person who knew what Bea kept in that safe. He would have taken the information to his grave had Mom and I not told him Bea was killed for the contents."

"Mr. Hallett? Mr. Robert Hallett?"

The brothers turned to see it was a doctor who was paging Robbie. Jay grabbed Cindy's hand and they walked over to find out the test results.

"I'm Robert Hallett. This is my older brother, Jay."

"Your Mom took a severe blow to the back of the head. She has a fractured skull with some swelling of the brain. X-ray did not pick up any cranial bleeding, which is a good thing."

"Is she going to be okay?" asked Robbie, choking on the words.

Jay put his arm around his brother's shoulders. Robbie was closer to their Mom and always had been; he was the youngest and a Momma's boy.

"We have placed her in an induced coma. We need to monitor the swelling and wait for it to go down before we can see if there is any permanent damage. She will stay in ICU, resting, until it does," answered the doctor.

"Can we see her?" Jay requested.

"You can visit with her for short periods of time. Family only. What she really needs is to rest and heal. I'll have the nurse tell you when she's settled into ICU and you can check in on her."

"I'm really sorry," said the doctor, shaking their hands and leaving.

"If there's any permanent damage…" Robbie choked out, tearing up.

"You have to think positive," Cindy suggested, grabbing his hand to squeeze it.

"Cindy, would you stay with Robbie? I'm going to tell the others Mom's progress so they can all go home," Jay requested.

"Sure. Come on, Robbie. Let's get a cup of that wonderful tasting coffee from the vending machine," Cindy offered with a painful smile.

Jay gave a report on his mother's injury to the folks in the waiting room, leaving out the fact that she was hit in the head with a rolling pin. He told them she was found in the walk-in with spilt chowder around her and left it at that. He thanked everyone for coming to the hospital and promised he would keep them all updated on her condition.

Everyone left but Cindy, who handed Jay a cup of coffee when he returned to her side. They sat in the corner waiting to hear from the nurse.

"I wonder if your Mom saw who hit her?" asked Cindy, breaking the silence.

"Or, if she knows why she was hit?" added Robbie.

"We won't know for a while I'm afraid," said Jay, sitting back in the uncomfortable chair.

Chapter 11

AFTER THEY CHECKED on Martha in ICU and stayed the allotted twenty minutes, the brothers decided to return to work knowing there was nothing they could do for their Mom but let her rest. Cindy left for The Burger Box promising she would call Jay later in the day.

Robbie didn't want to return to work right away. He asked Jay if it was okay that he come back in an hour or so; he wanted to walk the beach and have some quiet time to himself. Jay told him to take the whole day off if he wanted to. He also invited his younger brother to stay at his place so they would be together should any phone calls come in, and Robbie agreed.

The café was hopping when Jay got back. Kathy told him that everything was running smoothly. She had just taken Angie for a walk on her break and gave her treats when they had returned to the office. The hostess also informed him that Chief Boyd was out back with Officer Nickerson. Jay headed straight to the kitchen to see what was going on and why the Chief had returned. Yellow tape, once again, hung in the kitchen.

"Jay, you need to see this; Susan spotted it and called me," said Boyd.

They walked under the tape and to the far corner of the walk-in. Boyd pointed to a spot on the floor. A 'T' had been drawn into the spilt clam chowder.

"Do you think my Mom did this before she passed out?" Jay asked the Chief.

"I don't know. Susan said she and Josh came in to get some

seafood for the line and Josh almost stepped on it. She didn't think anyone else had been in there since the accident. Everyone had been using the back refrigerator because of the spill."

"Could that be the first letter of the name of whoever attacked her?"

"Do you have employees whose names start with 'T'?" asked Nickerson.

"Unfortunately, quite a few. I have two Tonys, a Terry, a Thomas, and a Tonya," Jay replied.

"And a partridge in a pear tree," finished Tom Nickerson. "Sorry… it just came out."

"Nickerson, you idiot," Boyd said, shaking his head.

"It's okay, Tom. I thought it was funny," Jay announced, smiling. "It so fit the moment."

"Jay, do you have time to catch me up now on what you found out instead of tomorrow?" asked the Chief.

"Sure, let's go to my office," suggested Jay. "It's quieter there."

"I'm out of here, Chief. Jay, I'm sorry about what happened to your Mom. She's going to be okay, I can feel it," said Tom, patting Jay on the back. "Don't worry…"

"I'll be in the office," Jay informed Kathy on his way by the hostess station.

"Hello, Stormy," the Chief greeted her when the dog met them at the door.

"Actually, it's Angie," Jay corrected.

"Whose Angie?" Boyd asked in confusion.

"The dog. Her real name is Angie. She belonged to George Peterson."

"How did you ever find that out?" he asked, sitting down.

Jay told him about the visit to Plymouth. He took out the letters he had received upon George's death and gave them to his friend to read. The Chief scratched his chin in puzzlement.

"With this new information, we could be looking at several

suspects working together," he said. "Jay, I for one, will be real glad when those cameras are installed on Monday."

"I know, so will I. If you look at all the evidence together it suggests that it must be one of the family members. But, which one and who are they posing as?"

Angie sat up and started to growl. Chief Boyd's eyes opened wide and he continued to stare at a spot in the corner of the room. Jay turned around to see Roland standing there.

"Roland, this is Chief Boyd," said Jay. "Chief Boyd, Roland Knowles."

"I saw the picture in the paper," stuttered Boyd. "But I thought it was just a publicity stunt."

"Roland, did you see who hit my Mom?" asked Jay.

The ghost nodded his head yes.

"Watch the cellar. Quiet is as quiet does…" could be heard as he vanished.

"What the heck is that supposed to mean?" asked the Chief, still not believing what he had just witnessed.

"I think he's trying to tell me to put cameras in the cellar, too," said Jay. "I didn't bother because there's only one way in and one way out."

"What's down cellar besides storage?" asked the Chief.

"The wine locker is there along with canned food and paper products. We don't even use half the cellar, it's so big."

"Why wouldn't he just tell us the name of who hurt your mother?"

"He has his reasons, I'm sure," answered Jay. "He's watching what's going on, too. I think he's trying to protect his hidden treasure from whoever it is trying to find it."

"You talk like you know this guy, ah…ghost," said Boyd. "Just how often do you talk to him?"

"Enough," was Jay's cryptic response.

"You really think this has to do with the Knowles' treasure?"

"I think it has everything to do with the treasure," said Jay, frowning. "People will do anything if it comes down to millions of dollars."

"True. Can you make me copies of these letters and drop them off at the station?"

"Sure. Tomorrow okay?" Jay offered.

"That's fine," answered the Chief as he stood up to leave.

Angie walked beside him to the door on his way out. The Chief patted her on the head and left.

She returned to her comfy bed and continued her interrupted nap. Jay finished entering the payroll into the computer, then he sat back in his leather chair, staring out the window.

Jay had never bargained for all of this when he opened his café. The Knowles' treasure never actually entered his mind when he had purchased the property. Sure, they had searched for the treasure when he was young, but it was a game back then. What was the poem his Dad taught him and his friends when they walked the beach under the point?

> One step forward,
> Two steps back,
> Watch out for the pirates, they'll give you a whack.
> False walls to the front,
> Dirt under your feet,
> Light up the lanterns,
> Through tunnels, you'll creep.
> An underground lighthouse,
> Will lead the way,
> To gems and gold,
> That will enrich your day.

It had been years since he thought about that poem; it was a wonder he even remembered it. Was it something that had a ring of truth to it or was it something made up in past years to enhance the story of the hidden treasure for tourists who visited the lighthouse? Jay wondered how many other people would recall the poem now that the picture of Roland's ghost had surfaced. Suddenly, there was a light rap on the office door.

"Come in," he called out as Angie opened one eye to see who it was.

Robbie entered the room, his eyes red and swollen.

"Jay, I'm going to do the liquor order and then go back to my place. I can't focus and I look like crap to be waiting on customers," he said. "I called Tucker and asked him to come in and cover for me."

"Another 'T' I forgot about," mumbled Jay. "Are you sure you want to do the ordering?"

"Yea, most of it is done down cellar so no one will see me."

"Okay. Write up the order and I'll put it in the computer when you're done so you can go home," insisted Jay. "You can sleep up in my room. Angie and I will sleep on the pull-out couch. There's beer in the fridge."

"Thanks, dude. I'm not like you. I'm not a strong person," said Robbie, tearing up again. "Especially when it comes to Mom." Suddenly, Robbie stiffened up and looked to his right. A hand was there on his shoulder; he could see it. He looked past the hand to a face that was sad.

"Jay..." whispered Robbie nervously.

"Robbie, meet Roland," said Jay, waiting for his brother to freak out.

"Martha will be okay..." said the ghost, fading away.

"You finally got your wish! You saw Roland. What do you think?" Jay asked with a chuckle.

"I liked it better when I couldn't see him," Robbie admitted, walking out the door.

"Some watch dog you are," said Jay reaching for Angie's leash. "You slept right though Roland's visit. Let's go for a walk before I have to go back to work."

Chapter 12

ROBBIE GRABBED HIS clipboard from underneath the bar. It was where he had last left it, untouched by the ghost. He was glad because he was in no mood to play hide and seek today. He did a quick look over the stock at the bar and headed for the cellar.

He counted the wine bottles already out of boxes and then the full boxes next to the wine locker. Next, he moved on to the hard liquor. He looked around, swearing he heard someone moving. His nose picked up the scent of smoke. Dropping the clipboard, he ran behind the locker to check the side of cellar not used.

"Don't fire me, man. I really need this job to help my Mom," Josh begged, stepping out of the shadows.

"What are you doing down here?" questioned Robbie. "I smell smoke."

Josh held out a pack of cigarettes. Robbie looked around at the floor; it was littered with butts that had been ground into the dirt floor. The young man had moved several empty crates to make himself a seat.

"I asked you a question. What are you doing down here?" repeated Robbie.

"My Mom is fighting cancer right now. If she knew I still smoked, she'd kill me. I can't take the chance of anyone seeing me outside the restaurant smoking. Everyone in town knows me and they'd run right to my Mom to tell her. On my breaks, I come down here to have a smoke. I always make sure the cigarettes are out by grinding them into the dirt."

"Don't you think you should have asked someone if it was all right?" asked Robbie. "You could have burned the place down."

"I'm always really careful. I need this job; I would never jeopardize the café. My money helps to buy my Mom's medicine," insisted Josh.

"I'm going to have to talk to Jay about this," Robbie advised him. "No more smoking down here until I do and he makes the decision if it's okay or not."

"Okay, I won't," said Josh, brushing past Robbie. "My break's over, I need to get back to the line."

Robbie watched the cook head back up the stairs. He wondered if smoking was the only thing he was doing down in the cellar. What if he was down there looking for the treasure? Maybe, Josh was the one who whacked his Mom. He walked around looking for footprints in the dirt; there were too many to tell who had walked where before.

He decided to finish the order and go talk to his brother before he left for the day. The clipboard had disappeared again.

"Aww, come on, Roland," he yelled throwing his hands up in the air. "What have I ever done to you?"

Roland hovered in the back corner of the cellar, smiling smugly.

Jay was walking the floor visiting his customers as Robbie flagged him over to the bar. The two brothers stood at the far end of the bar as Robbie told him the order was missing along with the clipboard. Jay chuckled. Robbie assured his older brother that they could go one day without ordering liquor and he would be in early the next morning to do another order. Roland usually returned the clipboard to under the bar when he was done with his joking around.

They then discussed Josh's smoking down cellar. Jay shared Robbie's concern that it might not be the only reason he was actually down there. They decided Jay would talk to the cook and tell him no more smoking down cellar and both brothers agreed to keep a closer eye on him. Robbie finally left for the day.

The dinner hour that night was steady; summer was now in full swing. Dinner rush was a little later as people were on the beach and took the time to go home and shower before coming to eat. The last customers finally left at ten forty-five. The dining areas were reset and Pam and Tucker restocked the bar for the following day. When all the staff was gone, Jay closed out the computers for that night and cleaned out the register drawer. He had let Angie out of the office to roam the restaurant and stretch her legs.

A soft voice in his ear alerted him to check the cellar; he had learned the hard way that Roland's warnings had to be taken seriously. Jay looked around for Angie, but he couldn't find her. He headed for the cellar calling out for the dog and noticed that the door was open. He snapped on the first set of lights at the top of the stairs and could hear frightened whining from below.

"Angie, where are you girl?" he asked stepping slowly down the stairs looking around.

Jay was halfway down to the cellar when the lights suddenly flickered and went out. Someone grabbed his ankles from between the wooden stairs and yanked him off balance. Jay plunged down the stairs and landed at the bottom at the bottom as someone jumped over him and ran up the stairs. He heard the cellar door lock with a click.

Angie was silent in the sudden stillness; Jay had to find her to make sure she was okay. He ran his hands along the wall to find the lower set of lights. Even with the cellar lights on, Jay still couldn't see the golden anywhere.

"Angie, where are you?" Jay cried out in fear.

Angie began whimpering quietly again. She could obviously hear Jay's voice, but couldn't go to him. Her owner followed her frightened whines to the wine locker. He opened the door and the golden sprang out in a sudden flash of fear.

He sat on the floor hugging the dog tightly. She jumped all over Jay, sloppily kissing his whole face and neck. Jay checked her over carefully to make sure she hadn't been hurt by whoever had locked her up.

"Now," he said to Angie. "We just have to get out of here. I sure wish I hadn't put three locks on the door."

Angie timidly followed her owner to the top of the wooden stairs. The cellar door was securely locked from the kitchen side. The dog scratched heavily on the door with her paw trying to get out, but Jay knew the door was too sturdy to break through.

"Roland, if you can hear me, go get Robbie. He's in the keeper's cottage. Tell him we need help," yelled Jay into the empty air.

There was no response. Jay decided he was not going to sit and do nothing. He went searching for clues to see if he could figure out who was down in the cellar and what they had been doing. He also realized that there had to be at least two people working together: one had shut off the lights at the top of the stairs and the other one had grabbed his feet from under the stairs. This was getting very complicated.

***

ROBBIE HAD DECIDED to take some medicine to get rid of his tension headache. He laid down on his brother's bed and dozed on and off waiting for the meds to finally kick in. He was having a strange dream that the covers were being pulled off the bed. As he opened his eyes, he realized it wasn't a dream at all. Roland was standing near the footboard. After he shook off his initial fear of seeing the ghost standing there, he told him to go away and pulled the pillow over his head.

"*Get out of bed...Jay needs your help,*" the voice in

Robbie's head demanded.

"What's happened to my brother?" Robbie questioned, sitting up, not afraid anymore.

"Go to the cellar."

Robbie jumped out of the bed and ran right through Roland to get out the door. He turned on the flood lights that faced the café. Not even taking the time to put on his shoes, he sprinted all the way to the café. He found that the front door was locked up tight.

Pulling out his key ring, it took several attempts to find the right key in the shadows. He pushed open the door yelling his brother's name, but there was no answer.

Roland said in the cellar.

He bolted through the kitchen to the locked cellar door. Peering around the surrounding area, he made sure that no one was around to ambush him or lock the cellar door behind him. The back door to the loading dock was open and swinging in the night breeze blowing in off the water.

Robbie unlatched the three hasp locks and cautiously opened the door. He saw that the lights were on in the lower cellar.

"Jay?" he yelled turning on the upper set of lights. "Jay, are you down there?"

"Robbie, bring a flashlight down with you," his older brother answered. "There's one on the bottom shelf of the bookcase in the kitchen office."

Tail wagging happily, Angie scrambled over to Robbie when his foot hit the bottom stair. Jay was sitting on some crates examining something that he had in his hand.

"What happened, dude? Roland said you needed help and he scared the hell out of me. I thought you were hurt."

"I did need help. I was locked in the cellar," Jay answered testily.

"Did you see who did it?"

"No, I didn't. I let Angie out of the office to roam around while I finished the night deposit. When I was done, I couldn't find her."

"Where was she?"

"Whoever was down here searching for the treasure locked her in the wine locker. The intruder must have left the door open and she heard him. Angie either knew who it was and came down on her own or was called down," said Jay, looking up from what he had in his hand.

"Dude, your face," said Robbie as he got closer to his brother.

Blood was trickling down his cheek from a gash above the right cheekbone. His shirt was filthy and ripped from his unfortunate fall down the stairs.

In his panic to find Angie, he hadn't realized that his cheek had been slashed when he face- planted on the wooden stairs.

"There were two of them," Jay confided.

"Two?"

"One at the top of the stairs who turned out the lights, and one hiding under the stairs who grabbed my ankles and sent me flying," answered Jay. "But, the one under the stairs made a big mistake."

"What kind of mistake?"

Jay held up a gold pocket watch.

"I found it under the stairs. In his haste of trying to escape quickly, whoever it was dropped it and didn't realize that he had."

"Is it real gold?" asked Robbie, inching closer to take a look at it.

"If I'm not mistaken, it's Roland Knowles' watch that was stolen from the safe at the historical society. It looks just like the one in the portrait of him I saw the first day I visited Bea."

"So, that means whoever killed Bea is now working here. Just wonderful..." Robbie concluded, shaking his head in disgust.

"This could definitely work to our advantage. Whoever dropped the watch doesn't know thatI found it. They're going to have to come back looking for it," Jay stated. "Security cameras won't be installed until Monday, and the whole staff knows that. But, if we hide a few personal recording devices in well-placed areas throughout the cellar, we might just catch the perpetrator searching under the stairs for it."

"I have one that I use to record my surfing. It has a timer so we can set it to start early in the morning. It records for eight hours on slow speed," Robbie suggested.

My pocket watch...I thought it was gone forever.

The brothers strained to see through the darkness at the back of the cellar. Roland was pointing to the object in Jay's hand. They could hear his footsteps as the ghost approached them. He leaned in to get a closer look and a smile crossed his face.

"Are you sure it's yours, Roland?" asked Jay, holding up the watch.

Custom made...melted pirate's treasure.

"This was made from the treasure you found?" Robbie asked in astonishment.

Ship's picture...The Fallen Mist.

The front case of the gold watch had a finely detailed, raised image of a four-masted schooner at full sail. The back of the case was smooth and had been so well polished you could see yourself in the surface.

"Bea said you cried on the shore the morning after the wreck," Jay remembered. "She claimed you were the first one there to collect the bodies that washed in from the wreckage."

My fault...

"Why, Roland? Why was it your fault?" Jay questioned.

The light went out in the storm...Nothing to guide the ship away from the point.

"It was a horrific storm; the worst on record in over one-hundred years. You must have done everything in your power to keep the lighthouse working," Jay observed.

I let all those people die. I didn't deserve to be rewarded with treasure.

"You didn't *let* them die," Robbie insisted, feeling sorry for the ghost.

I commissioned the watch to remind myself every day of the fate that befell those I didn't protect.

"You were only human. I'm sure you did the best you could under the circumstances," said Jay.

No, I failed. Every day from the catwalk, I see little Colleen searching for her mother on the point. Unfortunately, we never found her missing body.

"She might have been washed out to sea," suggested Robbie.

No. All the other bodies washed ashore, but not hers. I searched for days and never found her.

"You can't blame yourself. You have to let go of the guilt after all these years," Jay comforted.

I can't.

"You helped me; you went and got Robbie when I was in trouble. That just proves you're a good person…ghost," said Jay.

The ghost nodded.

"You know what else, Roland? You must be a good person because Angie isn't growling at you anymore. She's watching your every move, but she's not growling."

The ghost nodded again.

Guard my watch…secret compartment…he didn't find it.

"What's in the secret compartment?" asked Jay, turning the watch over in his hand.

Find the treasure…

"You mean it's still here?" Robbie asked wide-eyed.

Promised Martha….

"Promised Martha what?"

Not to tell...

The ghost suddenly vanished. Jay and Robbie looked at each other in absolute surprise. Roland had just admitted that the treasure was still here! Now, it was even more important to find out who was behind the treasure hunting before they actually found it and got away with both the treasure and murder.

Jay shined the flashlight to check under the stairs to see if there were any other clues but came up empty. Robbie brought back his camera and hid it behind several bottles of wine on the opposite wall from the stairway. Anyone coming from or going into the cellar would be caught on film. They set it to start recording at six-thirty the next morning.

The brothers shut the lights off and locked the cellar, along with the loading dock door. The deposit bag was exactly where Jay had left it on the hostess station.

Back at the keeper's cottage, Jay stored the watch inside the secret safe he had installed when he moved in. Not even his brother knew about the safe. He cleaned up the cut on his face, but decided to shower in the morning; he was too exhausted to do anything but fall on the bed and go to sleep.

He pulled the queen-size bed out of the couch for him and the dog to sleep on. They settled in and Jay closed his eyes. His muscles were starting to ache from the fall he had taken in the cellar.

Guard the watch...it is the key to finding the treasure. Don't tell Martha I told you.

"I won't, I promise," he mumbled, rolling over to go to sleep.

Chapter 13

JAY WAS UP at the crack of dawn. After a morning run with Angie, he showered and left for the hospital to check on his Mom; her condition hadn't changed. He sat by her side for twenty minutes, talking to her and stroking her hand.

"I'm so sorry, Mom," he repeated, hanging his head. "I had no idea that any of this would happen. I didn't know how dangerous these people really were."

The doctor came in to check on Martha as Jay was sitting there. He confirmed that the swelling was gradually going down around her brain; a few more days of rest and it should be almost back to normal. At that point, they would slowly back off the medications she was receiving to keep her in the induced coma. Jay thanked the doctor heartily and stood up to leave.

"I'll be back tomorrow," he whispered leaning in to kiss his Mom on the cheek.

Jay walked to the elevator and the door opened as Robbie stepped out. Jay filled him in on the doctor's latest prognosis. Robbie nodded and told him he'd be back to work right after he visited with their Mom.

It was barely nine o'clock and Jay had to pick up the dog, bring her to the office, and set up the register and computers for the day's business. The kitchen was already busy with the preparations for the day's meals.

"Has anyone seen Josh?" yelled Susan.

"He went down cellar to get me a fifty-pound bag of onions," answered one prep cook passing by.

"I'll go find him," Jay offered, wanting to go see what he was doing in the cellar.

The lights were on, but the cellar was currently empty. A huge bag of onions was sitting on the floor beside the wine locker.

"Josh, are you down here?" Jay yelled out.

No answer.

Jay quickly grabbed the camera from behind the wine and let it rewind and then hit the play button. Several prep cooks had gone up and down the stairs with supplies. Peter came down and collected liquor for the bar, twice. Josh came down the stairs, but was never filmed going back up.

Jay was mad at himself; he realized they should have put more than one camera in the cellar last night. They had discussed it, but decided not to do it. He had been more interested in concentrating on the stairs to see who would be looking for the watch when they should have been filming the entire cellar.

He replaced the camera in its his hiding place and hit record once again. There had to be another way in and out of the cellar; that's the only way Jay could explain Josh's disappearance. But, why would he drop the onions in the middle of the floor? If he was hunting for the treasure he wouldn't want people to know that was what he was doing. He would have left the bag of onions on the pallet along with the rest of them.

The more Jay thought about it, the more he concluded that Josh had walked in on someone else searching. He obviously saw something or someone he shouldn't have seen; that's why the onions were just dropped in the middle of the floor. Jay was now concerned for his employee's safety.

"Mr. Hallett, are you down there?" yelled a female voice from the top of the stairs.

"I'm here," he called out.

Mary Chase shuffled down the stairs. Jay quickly picked up an order form for liquor to make it look like he was doing something productive.

"I'm leaving now; there's a triple batch of chowder in the walk-in. I had originally requested tomorrow off when I had my interview for the job. Is that going to be a problem with Martha still in the hospital?" she asked, looking down at the floor.

"No, it's okay. I'm going to train a second person tomorrow to make the chowder so you don't have to work every day. I don't know how long my Mom will be out so we need someone else to take her shifts," Jay explained. "I do appreciate your being here every day and covering her hours as much as you have."

"It's fine, I can sure use the extra money. I'm going back to school in the fall," she confided.

"That's great. What are you going to be studying?" Jay questioned.

"Marine archeology."

"Nice. There's a lot of job opportunities in that field," Jay observed. "I had a friend in college who studied that; he's now working on a salvage ship off the coast of Florida."

"I would love to work out of Woods Hole," Mary started, staring at the lone bag of onions on the floor. "It's close to home and they have a huge research area. I could sort of be a sunken ship librarian."

"Fancy job title," he said, noticing that she was staring at the onions. "I have to get back to this order since it has to be called in before noon. Thanks again for all your extra effort."

"Why are the onions on the floor in the dirt?" she asked.

"I put them there to remember to bring them upstairs for Amy," Jay replied.

"Okay, I guess," she said, shrugging her shoulders.

Jay turned away to pretend to continue counting bottles. Mary plodded up the stairs, pausing at the top to watch her boss for a few seconds and then left.

An eye watched Jay through a small hole from behind the

wall.

When is he going to leave?

Josh lay on the dirt floor behind the watching figure, his hands, mouth, and legs bound with duct tape; he had been knocked unconscious.

Hurry up and leave already. I need to get that camera.

"I'll let Robbie do this when he gets here," Jay said, thinking out loud. "I don't have a clue what I'm doing with this order."

He threw the order form on the table, picked up the bag of onions, and headed for the stairs. As soon as the owner was out of sight, a secret door opened in the dirt wall behind the wine locker.

A figure dressed in chef's clothing ran over to get the camera that he was sure he had been filmed on. He ripped out the cassette, wiped over the entire camera with a towel to get rid of his fingerprints, and replaced it in its hiding place. He closed the door to the concealed room after making sure his captive was still unconscious. Grabbing a few cans of stewed tomatoes, he calmly walked up the stairs and returned to his work. He passed right by Jay who had gone into the prep room.

"Here's your onions, Amy," said Jay throwing the bag on the table. "Have you seen Josh?"

"Word came in from the kitchen there was an emergency with his Mom and he left," said the prep cook, shaking her head. "It doesn't sound like Josh to do something like that, just up and leave without telling anyone. I don't know."

Robbie sauntered by the prep room door as he started his shift.

"I'm going downstairs to do the liquor order. Just wanted to let you know I was "in the building"," he said, posing in an imitation of Elvis.

Amy giggled. It was a well-known fact that she had a crush on Robbie; everyone knew, but she didn't know everyone knew.

She'd sit up on the point on her morning break and watch him surf. When he'd see her up there he would show off a little more than usual, doing fancy tricks on his board.

"You're order forms are down on the table," said Jay as Robbie walked away.

"Probably not now," Robbie replied, knowing Jay would understand what he was talking about.

"I'm going to the office and look up Josh's cell number and give him a buzz. I'll let you know if I learn anything," he said to Amy.

"Thank you, Mr. Hallett," she answered gratefully, slicing the fifty-pound bag of onions open to prep them for onion rings.

"Call me Jay," he said, walking out the door.

Kathy, his head hostess, was off on Mondays. Ellie Holt, second in command over the waitresses was standing at the podium on tired feet.

"It's really slow today," she informed her boss.

"There will be days like this," he answered. "It's like a hundred degrees outside. I'm sure everyone is at the beach; I sure would be if I wasn't working."

"Not me," she laughed. "I'd be at home in my backyard hiding from the tourists."

"You've been on the Cape too long," laughed Jay, heading off to the office. "If there's time, have the waitresses roll extra silverware and do some cleaning."

Jay went straight to the file cabinet to look up Josh's cell phone number. He dialed the number and it continued to ring with no one picking up; he hung up and tried again. It continued to ring hollowly. Maybe Josh was at the hospital and couldn't answer the phone. He hung up a second time, deciding he would try again in an hour or so.

Robbie burst head long into the office, out of breath.

"Jay, you have to come down cellar right now," his younger brother said, pulling him out of the chair behind the desk.

"What's going on?" he asked, allowing himself to be dragged along.

"I'll tell you when we get there," Robbie replied.

Robbie carefully led him to the rear of the cellar.

"Just listen," he said insistently.

The two brothers stood there in complete silence. After a few minutes, Robbie let out a huge sigh.

"What was I listening for?" asked Jay in confusion.

"I was standing over at the liquor shelves and I could have sworn I heard a phone ringing. Not once, but twice," asserted the younger brother.

"Where did it sound like it was coming from?"

"That's just it, I couldn't tell. I looked around for a phone, but couldn't find one anywhere."

"You say it rang twice?" asked Jay, putting two and two together then pulling out his own cell phone.

"What are you doing?" asked Robbie.

"Shhh," said Jay as he hit the redial button.

Suddenly, a phone started ringing quietly.

"That's it!" Robbie exclaimed. "Where is it coming from?"

Jay stepped towards the wall. He put his ear to the dirt surface directly in front of him.

"It's coming from behind this wall," he observed, startled.

"Who did you call?"

"It's Josh's cell phone. He disappeared about an hour ago when he came down here to get onions for Amy. The kitchen staff said he left for a family emergency. We have to find out who started that story, but first we have to find Josh," Jay proposed.

"How did he get behind the wall?" Robbie asked in consternation.

"There's got to be a hidden latch somewhere. Start looking,"

The two brothers ran their fingers over the wall inch by inch. Every few minutes, Jay had to redial the number to keep

Josh's phone ringing to guide them. They narrowed it down to one area where the ringing was the loudest. The brothers concentrated their fingers' searching to a five-foot section in front of them.

Robbie pushed on a small round stone. There was a loud click and the wall moved ever so slightly.

"Jay, over here," he called to his brother.

They discovered the slight opening in the wall. Together, they stuck their fingers in the seam and pulled. The wall swung open effortlessly and silently; the room beyond was totally dark.

"Grab a flashlight," Jay ordered, cautiously walking forward.

Robbie shined the beam of light into the room just as Jay was going to trip over the body on the floor.

"Oh, hell, it's Josh," Jay realized pulling the duct tape off his employee's mouth. "Let's get him off the cold floor."

They carried him out of the dark room and laid him down on the full boxes of liquor under better light. He started to stir as his lungs finally took in cleaner air. Thinking he was still with his captors, he started lashing out frantically, trying to get away. His eyes reflected pure panic and he started screaming as soon as he realized he no longer had the tape over his mouth.

"Josh, it's Jay and Robbie. Calm down now, you're okay. Stay still so I can get the rest of the duct tape off you," Jay ordered.

Josh just stared at Jay blankly. He stopped thrashing as soon as he recognized his boss' face. Robbie retrieved his pocket knife and cut the remaining tape off Josh's hands and feet. The young man sat up, rubbing his hands trying to get some feeling back in them.

"Who did this to you, Josh?" Jay asked commandingly.

"It was a guy in chef's clothing, but I didn't get to see his face. All I saw was the black and white checkered pants," Josh stuttered out.

A stifled scream hissed out from the direction of the stairs. The three men looked over to see Susan standing there with her hand clasped over her mouth.

"Oh, my God, Josh, what happened to you?" Susan asked as she slowly approached them.

"Just an accident," Josh answered.

"Are you okay?" she inquired.

"I'm fine," he quietly replied.

"Did you need something, Susan?" asked Jay.

"The security crew is here to install the cameras. They need to talk to you about where you want the cameras placed," she answered, staring at Josh.

"I'll be up momentarily," he instructed.

"Okay, I'll tell them," she agreed as she walked back up the stairs.

"You don't like her, do you, Josh?" asked Robbie.

"No!" he answered curtly.

"Why not?" Jay questioned.

"I don't trust her; she's too goody-goody," Josh answered. "She's nice and all, she just bothers me somehow. She has to be everybody's friend."

"Are you okay to walk?" asked Jay. "Let's get you out to the loading dock and get some fresh air into those lungs of yours."

"I found these on the floor in front of the onion pallet. I tucked them in my pocket right before I got whacked because they looked important. I was going to give them to you, Mr. Hallett, when I got back upstairs," Josh said, taking some folded papers out of his smock pocket.

Jay tucked them in his back pocket without looking at them. They helped Josh down off the boxes and back went upstairs. Robbie took him out to the loading dock while Jay went to deal with the security team who would be installing the security cameras.

They strolled around the kitchen and the loading dock areas

mapping out where the cameras would be installed for the best total coverage. They decided two cameras would be placed outside the back door, two inside on the loading dock, and four in the kitchen.

As they moved on to the cellar, Jay decided he wanted this area covered completely. Four cameras would be installed in the stock area: one facing the stairs, one pointing down the stairs into the cellar, one covering the liquor and wine stock, and one viewing the back side of the cellar not currently used.

A state-of-the-art monitoring system would be set up in Jay's office. Each camera would have its own monitor that would record what it was viewing 24/7. These, combined with the cameras already in place at the front of the café, would provide viewing of almost one hundred percent of the café.

The alarm crew was discussing how they would run the wires when Jay went to retrieve the portable camera that was hidden behind the wine. He picked it up and noticed that it had been turned off. Flipping open the side of the camera, he was pissed to find the cassette was gone.

"These people are always one step ahead of me," he grumbled angrily.

"Are you talking to us, Mr. Hallett?" asked the guy holding the map.

"No, I was talking to myself," he answered. "Do you need me for anything else?"

"I think we have everything we need to start. We'll come find you if we have any questions," the foreman informed him. "We do need access to your office to run wires, though."

"I'll leave the door open for you," Jay agreed.

No one was outside at the loading dock so Jay went in search of his brother and Josh.

"Are you looking for Robbie?" asked Susan as he stopped to look around the kitchen

"Yea, where'd they go?" he asked, palming the camera

hoping that no one would notice it.

"Robbie took Josh home to change his clothes. He said he wanted to keep working and that he said he couldn't lose any hours because of his Mom," Susan volunteered, glancing at the camera.

Jay took out his cell phone and texted Robbie to inform Josh to take the rest of today and tomorrow off with full pay. He could return to work the following day but only if he felt up to it. Robbie sent a message back that Josh agreed and that he would be back to work shortly to finish the liquor order.

Jay replied, asking him to stop at the office first.

As promised, Jay left the office door open as he placed the empty camera on the desk top. Next, he placed a call to Chief Boyd asking him to come to the café when he had a chance. As Jay leaned forward to turn on his computer, the folded papers that he had stuck in his back pocket crackled. He stood up and pulled the papers out to read them over.

It's probably just an invoice.

But turns out, the papers were not an invoice. He sat back down and slowly spread them out on his desk. They were birth certificates; the stolen certificates that had been in Bea's safe. He looked them over and deemed them to be the originals that were issued many years ago. He realized that these were evidence in Bea's murder and the Chief would probably confiscate them. Unfortunately, he had already handled them and so had Josh, which meant that both their fingerprints would be on the papers.

Jay made copies of both sides of each birth certificate so he would have all the information needed for his own research. He sent Ellie to the kitchen to get him four plastic bags, three for the certificates and one for the camera. He then placed another call to the Chief; this time he spoke directly to Boyd who indicated he would be there within the hour.

As Jay was examining the new evidence that had been given to him, Robbie popped his head in the door.

"You wanted to see me?" he asked. "Where's Angie?"

"I took her home because of the work being done around here today," he answered as he held up the camera in the plastic bag. "Someone took the cassette."

"Seriously?"

"Probably the same person who hit Josh," Jay speculated.

"So, we're back to square one," Robbie said, shaking his head in frustration.

"For now, but this afternoon all the cameras will be installed and recording every inch of this place," Jay said. The monitors and recorders will all be locked up in here. You and I are the only ones with the keys to this office."

"I wonder if Roland saw anything?" Robbie pondered.

I stay in the lighthouse…

The brothers turned around. Roland was hovering in the corner near the door that leads to outside.

He said to stay in the lighthouse.

"Roland, I have changed my mind. If you want to wander around during the day, go right ahead. If customers do see you, just be prepared for their reactions. If I hadn't asked you to stay in the lighthouse during working hours, you might have seen something when everyone was attacked," Jay added. "I should have a meeting with my employees and give them fair warning that you might be wandering around."

"Do you know anything about the secret room where we found Josh locked up?" asked Robbie curiously.

Many more…there are many more.

"Dude, can you not take my stuff anymore?" begged Robbie.

Roland smiled. The brothers could hear his laughter as the ghost faded away.

"For a ghost, he sure can be aggravating," said Robbie, frowning. "I'll be down cellar."

The first batch of wires had to be hooked up in the office.

Jay decided to head out and took the four plastic bags to wait for Chief Boyd in the front foyer. When he finally arrived, they went to the bar upstairs to have lunch and discuss the situation. It was midafternoon and Peter was the only one who was upstairs. He poured Jay a beer on tap and raised an eyebrow at the Chief. The Chief was on duty and couldn't drink so he had a soda instead.

"Man, that beer looks good. It's got to be a hundred out there. So, catch me up on what's been happening around here."

Jay caught his friend up on the current attack on Josh and ended with giving him the plastic bags, requesting an examination for fingerprints on all the items.

"By the way, do you know this person?" asked Boyd, placing a photo on the bar in front of Jay.

"I know of him, but not who he is?" Jay answered. "Why?"

"This is a picture taken on a video camera across the street from the historical society. Look hard at his clothes," instructed the Chief.

Jay picked up the photo and studied it closely.

"Is that blood on his shirt and pants?"

"Yea, we think this is Bea's killer. He was filmed leaving the back of the building the afternoon she died. You said you know of him?"

"I was eating at The Burger Box before the café opened. I saw Ty, my cook, slammed into the window outside the booth I was sitting in by this same man. They had harsh words and then each went their separate way."

"That's not much help. The one person connected to this guy is now dead. You haven't seen him since?" asked the Chief, digging into his lunch.

"No, I don't think he's from around here. Ty knew him and he was from Pennsylvania," answered Jay. "I don't think it would be much help anyway. I am almost positive that Tyrone Fenster was not his real name."

Robbie walked behind the bar and set the clipboard down

with a snap; he looked shaken.

"What's up, Robbie?" the Chief asked.

"The whole time I was down cellar I felt like someone was watching me," he explained.

"You sure it wasn't the ghost?" Boyd snickered.

"No, Roland doesn't scare me anymore, he just annoys me," Robbie replied. "This was like that hair standing up on the back of your neck feeling. Someone else was down there besides me."

"I think maybe we should go down cellar and check out this hidden room," suggested the Chief, pushing his lunch away from him. "Peter, I'll be back to finish this."

The brothers took the Chief to the false wall and opened up the door. This time, they each had a flashlight and the room was well lit. Four dirt walls and a dirt floor pretty much summed up the space. It appeared empty of anything else. Two peep holes dug into the dirt allowed whoever was hiding back there to watch the entire rear area of the cellar.

Boyd walked around, shining his flashlight on the dirt floor, then stopped at the far wall.

"Guys, come here and look at this," he said, kneeling down.

The dirt on the floor had a well-defined pattern of something being dragged across it repeatedly. The quarter circle swung out from the wall and stopped sharply at a ninety-degree angle.

"I think we have another door here," the Chief observed, standing up. "And, it looks like it's been opened recently."

It didn't take them long to locate the hidden latch. A long, dark corridor stretched before them as Boyd shone his flashlight beam down the tunnel. There were footprints in the dirt leading to and from the other end.

"Shall we find out where it leads to?" Jay asked, stepping into the opening.

"Try not to walk over the footprints. Hug the wall if you can," Boyd suggested.

The three men walked slowly into the darkness in single file.

If it wasn't for the existing footprints, the tunnel looked like it hadn't been disturbed in over a hundred years. The walls had been shored up with wooden timbers that looked like they had once been used in the hulls of ships. Small squares had been dug into the dirt walls between the timbers every twenty feet. They held items that must have washed ashore after each wreck. The tunnel was a hidden shrine to those ships and the souls that had been lost in the wrecks off the point.

"I don't see any treasure here," Robbie observed.

"If there was any, I'm sure the person using this tunnel took it already," Jay replied.

They haven't found the treasure.

"Roland, is this your tunnel? Did you do this?" Jay questioned.

Not mine...the souls lost to the sea.

"Did you do this to honor them?" Jay asked in confusion.

He took things...things that did not belong to him.

"We're at the end," Boyd noticed. "Do you want to open it up to see where we are?"

Turn off your lights. He's coming in.

The tunnel went dark as the three men stood in place, barely breathing. A loud click came from the wall and sunlight began to pour in as a large man pulled the heavy door open. He looked up and saw the three men staring at him. Panicking and pushing the door closed, he took off running.

"That's the guy in the picture," yelled the Chief bearing down on the door. "How the hell do you open this thing? Quick, he's getting away."

They looked for a spot on the wall where the dust had been previously disturbed. Robbie pushed on the same area and the familiar noise of a click could be heard. Boyd pushed through the door and ran off at full speed to see if he could catch the wanted suspect.

Jay and Robbie stayed behind, investigating the tunnel using the bright daylight that was streaming in from outside. A pile of flat rocks was piled up just inside the door. On top, sat a leather-bound journal. Jay picked it up and flipped through the pages.

"I think we just found Roland's stolen journal," Jay realized.

"That guy must have figured it would be safe here," said Robbie, looking over his brother's shoulder. "Cool…that looks like a map of the entire cellar."

"He was long gone before I got to the parking lot," said Boyd as he returned, breathing heavily. "I did talk to a couple who saw him drive away in a white truck that had Pennsylvania plates."

Jay slid the journal behind his back. He knew it was evidence and should be turned over to the Chief, but he wasn't done with it quite yet.

Chapter 14

BOYD LEFT TO put out an APB on the white truck and completely forgot about finishing his lunch.

Jay and Robbie walked outside to see exactly where the door came out of the cellar.

It had been dug into the dirt foundation underneath the base of the lighthouse. The suspect must have followed the maps in the journal and once he found the hidden entrance, he used it to get in and out of the cellar without being seen.

"He's working with someone in the kitchen, but who?" Jay said, thinking out loud.

"Why in the kitchen?"

"Josh said the only thing he saw on his captor was black and white checkered pants like a cook would wear," reasoned Jay. "Mom drew a 'T' in the spilt chowder; we have four people who work in our kitchen with first names who start with that letter and two with last names."

"I noticed that you hid the book from the Chief. Isn't that considered evidence in a murder?" Robbie inquired.

"After I take copies of all the pages, I'll be happy to turn it over to him. If he asks, I'll tell him I found it later in the day after he left," Jay answered. "I'll keep you out of it, Robbie."

"You really have changed," said the younger brother, shaking his head. "Attorney Jeremy would never have done something like this."

"Attorney Jeremy is gone," Jay replied stiffly.

"Do you think the suspect will actually come back for the

book?" Robbie questioned. "He has killed for it and as far as we know, it's the only thing he had to lead him to the treasure."

"I don't think he'll risk getting caught again. His inside partner will be the one to try to get it back. We should figure out some way to block off this end of the tunnel," Jay suggested. "We need to get back to the cellar and close off the secret room before anyone else discovers it, if they haven't already."

"I called in the liquor order. Since this was supposed to be my day off. I think I'll go get in a couple of hours on the board," Robbie decided. "Then, I'm going to visit Mom again in the hospital."

"Okay, I'll take care of things around here. See you tomorrow," Jay responded, studying the door trying to figure out how to keep it from opening again.

He couldn't block the door off from the outside as it would interfere with people walking from the parking lot to the lighthouse. He decided he would have to block it off on the other end inside the cellar. He could stack pallets against the door to the hidden room so that it couldn't be accessed from the tunnel. He hoped there were no other entries into the cellar from the outside that he was unaware of.

Jay felt disheartened that he couldn't protect the shrine that Roland had created in the passageway. There was a lot of history contained in those make-shift shelves lining the dirt walls. He hoped the bad guy wouldn't come back later in the night, find the book gone, get mad and destroy the historical displays.

If only the door swung in, but it doesn't.

He turned on his flashlight again and pulled hard on the door to close it tight. He thought he heard a grinding noise coming from underneath the door. Thinking the door was stuck on a small rock, he kicked at the dirt. A small, flat irregular shaped piece of metal was shining through the soil. Jay bent down, picked it up, and examined it closely. He brushed off as much dirt as he could, but the crevices were still caked with hard soil.

He dropped to his knees to sift through the dirt but found nothing else.

Putting the object in his pocket, he headed back to the hidden room.

Checking the cellar to make certain that no one else was around, Jay dragged six empty pallets into the room behind the wall and pushed them up against the door that lead to the tunnel. He closed the door just before the security crew came traipsing down the stairs to finally install the cellar cameras.

He had to rush home to change his clothes since the new cook was coming in to learn how to make the chowder in about an hour. Poor Angie had been locked up in the house by herself all morning. She would definitely need to go out to potty.

"What happened to you?" asked Ellie, washing the plastic covers of the menus.

"Oh, I was moving stuff around down cellar for the camera guys," Jay said, lying through his teeth. "I'm going home to change before the new cook comes in that I hired. I'll be back shortly."

Angie danced circles when Jay came in through the door. She definitely didn't like being left alone. He let her out the back door to do her business while he stood on the deck watching her. He reached around to his back to see if the journal was still there. He was going to lock it up in the safe along with the watch for safekeeping.

He decided that tonight he would sit and read through its pages. He had to find out if there were any other secret entrances into his building. Until he had that information, he couldn't properly protect his employees from any more attacks occurring.

"Come on, girl," Jay called out.

He gave the dog a new pig's ear to chew on. Changing his clothes, he reached into the front pocket of his pants to retrieve the object he had discovered in the tunnel. He stepped into the bathroom and ran it under the hot water to see if he could break up the dirt that encased the object. Years of build-up slowly melted away as the water streamed over it. It appeared to be some kind of coin.

Jay flipped it over and back, studying each side. Angie growled slightly and then settled back down to gnaw on her treat.

It's a gold doubloon, my boy...

Startled, Jay almost dropped the coin he was holding into the sink. Walking out into the bedroom, he searched for Roland; he didn't even care that he was standing there in just his underwear.

I must have dropped it in the tunnel...

"Is this part of your treasure?" Jay quizzed the ghost.

Yes, it would be...

"I found your journal. Whoever killed Bea had hidden it inside the tunnel. Is the treasure still here, Roland?" he asked.

It is...

"Do you mind if I read your journal?"

No.

"I'm going to call a meeting at the café first thing in the morning to inform my staff that you really do exist. It's not fair of me to say where you can go and not go on your own property. Be forewarned though, the first few times you are appear, my staff might freak out. People will undoubtedly come here looking for you once word gets out."

Roland nodded solemnly.

"I'm not going to promise you that I won't look for the treasure, at least at some point. It would be unbelievable to be able to open a museum in the smaller building behind the café. I would love to close off the walls of your tunnel behind glass so people can see the history you have captured down there."

Do not speak of the treasure. Not now.

"That will be something between me, my bother, and my Mom," answered Jay.

Have to go…

Roland walked into the wall and was suddenly gone. Jay set the coin on the journal and changed into clean clothes. He traipsed downstairs and locked the two valuable items up in his safe. Clipping on Angie's leash, they left for the café together.

Jay worked in his office with Angie while the alarm experts finished wiring the monitors. The newly hired cook strangely never showed up for the first day of work. Jay called his cell phone several times and left messages, but he never received an answer back.

The alarm company finally finished and left around five. Jay strolled around the café, carefully checking out the camera placement. The upstairs cameras were wireless while the cameras down cellar had been hard wired. Jay returned to his office and sat there watching the monitors; there was nowhere he couldn't observe in his café. He concentrated his attention on the monitor that covered the back of the cellar.

Roland abruptly appeared on the screen. He floated around a bit like he couldn't decide what he wanted to do; it was almost like he was pacing. He finally disappeared into the wall at the far-left corner of the cellar.

I'll have to be sure and check that area for hidden doors.

Supper rush was in full swing. Since the new chowder cook hadn't shown show up, a new batch for tomorrow had not been made. He went to the walk-in to check to verify just how much was left. It had been a slow lunch so luckily there was a full bucket to open with tomorrow. Mary would be in early enough to complete a new batch for supper tomorrow night.

He covered Ellie's break at the hostess station and noticed that people were enjoying cocktails in the waiting area and walking around outside in the cool evening air. Suddenly, a loud crash pierced the air from the second floor. Jay took the stairs two at a time. Janet, one of the waitresses, was standing shaking at a table next to the roped off telescope and a tray of food was on the floor. Jay hustled over to try and calm people down.

"Jay, he's here. There's really a ghost. I saw him, and so did they," Janet confessed in alarm, pointing to the customers at her table.

"We did. We saw him, too," the woman confessed.

"I didn't see anything," her husband said, returning to his salad.

"Let's clean up this mess and get our customers some new food, on the house," Jay suggested.

"I don't know if I want to eat here now," the wife stated uncertainly.

"Oh, just be quiet and wait for your food. It's on the house," her husband demanded sharply. "I'm not leaving here and I am the one with the car keys."

Jay and Janet cleaned up the mess and returned to the kitchen where Jay ordered the same meals to be prepared again. "Small accident," he explained to the cooks. With a wink, he pulled Janet in to the corner and told her he knew about the ghost. Her eyes grew wide as she listened to him talking matter-of-factly about it. He assured Janet that Roland wouldn't hurt her and that there would be a meeting tomorrow morning to explain everything to the entire staff.

Jay questioned her if she would be okay for the rest of the night; she said yes, it had just caught her off guard.

Susan paged Janet to tell her the food was ready to be served again. She loaded the tray up and hustled out of the kitchen.

"Is it true?" Susan asked Jay under her breath.

"Is what true?"

"Several of the waitresses came back and said Janet had seen saw the actual ghost," Susan answered.

"That's what she described," Jay confirmed, being very vague.

"So, the rumors are true," she confirmed, placing a plate up under the warmer.

"Rumors?"

"Yea, ghosts and treasure," she admitted, staring at him.

"Jay, Peter needs you at the bar," Ellie called through the kitchen door.

"Have to go," Jay informed her, glad for a reason to end the uncomfortable conversation.

Roland didn't appear again the rest of the night. The restaurant closed at ten. Jay called a quick meeting to advise the staff of Roland's existence. He pondered as he watched them leave, just how many of his employees would return to work the following day.

Alone in the café, Jay emptied the register while Angie scampered around the first floor. He had put a chair in front of each kitchen door to keep her confined to the area where he was working. He grabbed her leash and the deposit bag and they jogged home.

The moon was almost full, Jay noticed as he stood on the back deck of the cottage looking out over the ocean enjoying a beer. He loved summer nights on Cape Cod. Angie was inside, not allowed out at night because of free-roaming coyotes in the area. She lay just inside the screen door watching his every move.

The point was well lit due to the shining moon. Suddenly, something moved far off in the distance. Jay squinted to see who or what is was. Three dark figures, side by side, were walking along the path above the cliffs, and then suddenly, they were gone.

I thought they were only seen down by the water's edge.

He got a chill over his whole body despite the fact that not a wisp of wind was stirring. History was coming to life and he was a witness to it all. Perhaps the three pirate ghosts hadn't been seen in recent years because the property had been abandoned; there had been no one here to see them still roaming the point.

Jay wondered if these were the three crew members who

had been killed by the captain and left behind to guard the treasure as legend indicated. He wondered if they were protecting the same treasure that Roland Knowles had found or was there more unaccounted for treasure on the point?

So many unanswered questions ran through Jay's mind all at once. He was simply too tired to look through the journal tonight to try to find some of those answers. Friday was his day off; he would take the book down to the beach and let Angie run for a few hours while he read. He locked up the house for the night and called the dog to go upstairs to go to bed.

In the middle of the night, Jay was awakened by the alarm going off inside the café. He jumped into his jeans and a muscle shirt, threw the leash on Angie, and sprinted to his restaurant in panic. The front was locked up tight; he ran around to the loading dock area with the dog in tow. The back door had been pried open by someone. Robbie came running up right behind his brother, breathing heavily.

"Have you been inside yet?" Robbie asked.

"No, I haven't. You stay here and guard the back door in case someone gets by me. Do you want Angie to stay with you?"

"Yea," Robbie replied.

Jay handed off Angie's leash and disappeared quickly inside the open door. The area was immediately flooded with light. Sirens could be heard coming up the hill; the alarm company must have automatically notified the police. Officer Nickerson came around to the back of the café with his weapon drawn.

"It's me," Robbie yelled out desperately when he saw the moonlight reflect off the gun in his friend's hand.

Tom Nickerson slowly lowered his weapon then he walked around Robbie and peered into the door that stood ajar.

"Where's Jay?" the officer wanted to know.

"He went inside and told me to stay and watch the door," Robbie answered.

"Robbie, you can come in, there's no one here," Jay called

out from inside the kitchen.

"Hey, Tom," he greeted the officer who was holstering his gun.

"You didn't see anyone?" Tom asked, looking around.

"It's weird. The cellar door is still locked and the two chairs I placed against the kitchen doors are still in place; it's like no one was even in here," Jay commented.

"Do you think the alarm scared them away?" Robbie asked.

"Could have. But, if the culprit was someone who worked here or they are working with someone who works here, they would certainly have known about the alarm," Jay affirmed.

"It's like they set the alarm off and then ran," Tom said.

Jay, go home.

All three men heard the warning in the air, loud and clear. Tom looked around, totally confused, as the voice dissipated.

"The journal," Jay yelled, taking off at a run. "Robbie, stay here with Angie."

"What was that?" Tom asked, turning to the younger brother. "Where's he going?"

"The keeper's cottage. Please, go help him," Robbie urged.

The officer bolted after Jay in time to see that Jay had arrived at the front door of his home which was standing wide open. He stopped to listen carefully; he could hear someone upstairs. Tom raced up behind him, stopping on the other side of the door. Jay put his finger up to his lips as they heard items hitting the floor above them. Tom slowly withdrew his gun from the holster.

"Stay behind me," he ordered.

They stepped into the living room and observed that the room had been trashed. They listened carefully and could hear footsteps moving from room to room upstairs. Tom waved Jay to one side of the stairway.

"This is the police. Come on down with your hands where I can see them."

The footsteps stopped suddenly and Jay heard his bedroom window open.

"The window; he's going out the back," Jay yelled, taking off.

Tom followed closely behind. They turned the corner just in time to see a figure jumping into the sand to the side of the deck. The intruder scrambled off into the dark.

"I'm headed around to the front," the officer yelled, as Jay loped around the deck.

Tom was racing by the front door when a second figure came barreling out of the house. He smashed into the police officer on purpose, knocking him off his feet, and then charged off down the hill. Tom let out a yell of pain as he hit the ground. Jay heard his friend struggling and gave up on the chase, jogging back to the front of the house.

"There were two of them," Tom confirmed, rubbing his leg.

"Are you hurt?"

"Yea, I landed pretty hard on my bad knee," he responded in pain.

Jay helped his friend up and they limped into the house together. The second floor had been totally trashed; the two suspects had managed to do a lot of damage in just a short period of time.

"What were they looking for?" Tom wondered.

"Something I found in the tunnel today that they were hiding there for safekeeping," Jay answered. "Roland Knowles' journal."

"The one from the historical society robbery?" Tom asked incredulously.

"Yea, the one from Bea's safe," Jay confirmed. "Luckily, I had locked it in my own safe before I headed off to bed."

"When were you going to turn it over to Boyd?" Tom wanted to know.

"Tomorrow. Between you and me, I wanted a chance to

photocopy the pages so I could protect my employees better. I need to know about all the secret access tunnels to get into the building and there are several maps drawn in the journal illustrating them."

"Crap. We forgot about Robbie over at the café," Jay remembered. "Will you stay here at the house while I go lock up the café?"

"Sure. I don't think they'll be back though."

Jay set off to relieve Robbie of guard duty at the café. His younger brother and the dog were sitting in the kitchen, sharing a hearty roast beef sandwich.

"I should have known when I didn't get greeted at the door," Jay observed, chuckling.

"Midnight snack. What can I say? We were both hungry," Robbie confessed, giving the dog another hunk of roast beef.

Robbie wrapped the remainder of the sandwich in a paper towel and stuck it in his sweatshirt pocket for later. They secured the café again and reset the alarm. The loading dock door would have to be replaced, but it could still be used for tonight. Walking back to the cottage, Jay told Robbie what had really happened; the café had been a diversion so they could search the keeper's cottage for the missing journal.

Jay also told his brother something else that he hadn't told Tom. There was something familiar about the person he was chasing through the dark. He couldn't put his finger on what is was, but he hoped it would come to him soon.

"I sure hope they didn't hit my place," Robbie despaired.

"I don't think they had time," Jay replied. "But just to be sure your place is secure, I'll ask Tom to escort you home and check out your cottage."

Tom was perched on the front porch step when the brothers got back from the café, still rubbing his knee. Standing up, he kept as much weight as he could off the injured leg.

"I was going to ask you to walk with Robbie back to his

cottage, but looking at you standing there, I don't think I will," said Jay. "Would you mind sitting there a few more minutes while I go check out his cottage with him?"

"Yea, go ahead," Tom agreed sitting down heavily again.

Ten minutes later, Jay was back. He walked Tom over to the patrol car.

"Make sure you turn that journal over to the Chief tomorrow," he advised, getting in the car. "I didn't see a thing tonight. Literally."

"Get that leg x-rayed," Jay suggested. "You can't always blame everything on an old football injury."

Back at the cottage, Jay automatically locked the front door.

"A lot of good that's going to do with the glass broken out of the window," he commented to the dog. "What say we just crash on the couch? At least we'll be downstairs."

The next morning, Jay called to have someone come repair the window in his front door. He also called to have a replacement door delivered and installed at the café. Next, he went upstairs to survey the damage; the office seemed to have sustained the worst of it. Every drawer had been emptied, every shelf cleared, and every picture ripped off the wall looking for the hiding spot for the journal.

"When I get my hands on who did this," Jay muttered, talking to Angie who was busily sniffing around the window.

I wasn't here...I didn't see until it was too late.

"It's okay, Roland; you can't be everywhere. We all thought they were in the café," Jay responded, picking piles of stuff up off the floor and setting it all back on the desk.

"I just wish I could figure out who my back-stabbing employee is."

Uncle and nephew...

"Did you say uncle and nephew?"

Family...my family. He had my journal.

"Who are they, Roland? Do you know their names?" Jay

questioned.

Redmond...all I heard was Redmond.

"I know that name; it's on one of the birth certificates I gave to the Chief," Jay acknowledged. "Redmond Jules, Jr. was Bea's son. It's not a very common name."

Angie was still sniffing around the window that the first intruder had jumped out of the night before. Something was keeping her interest. Roland once again disappeared into the wall.

"Want to go for a ride, girl? We need to pay a visit to the Chief," Jay offered, pulling out his cell phone. "Robbie, can you come over to the cottage? I need to go to town and the handyman is coming to replace the window. Thanks."

Summer was in full swing in the center of town. It was drizzling off and on which unfortunately made for a lousy beach day. The tourists had turned to shopping since they couldn't soak up the sun. The café would definitely be busy today because of the weather.

Jay drove up and down Main Street, twice, trying to find a parking place. He finally found a car pulling out of a spot. He turned on his directional and was waiting for the car to leave, when he noticed a white pick-up with Pennsylvania plates passing him and heading in the opposite direction. Driving it, was the man who had opened the tunnel door.

Chapter 15

JAY WAITED FOR an opening in the traffic and then he nosed his vehicle across the road in a K-turn. Horns blared and people yelled out their car windows at him as he smoothly executed the maneuver. He didn't care; he had to follow that white truck and see where it went.

He could see the roof of the truck as it traveled to the end of Main Street and made a right at the lights heading towards the beach. Jay got stuck at the red light; he made the right turn and then drove slowly along Beach Road. Most of the houses were seasonal rentals. This time of year, every house was occupied. Half way down to the dead-end, Jay saw the truck pull into a large garage which was attached to a green two-story house.

He drove on to the dead-end and pulled out his cell phone to contact the Chief. He explained what was happening and where he was. Boyd told him to stay put in his vehicle and wait until they got there. Jay could see the opening off the garage from where he had parked. Two police cars pulled up in front of the house as Jay pulled forward and parked across the street.

Boyd and Nickerson walked up to the front door and knocked vigorously. It was answered by the barking of a dog and a young man dressed in sweats.

"Where is Redmond Jules?" Boyd demanded to know.

"Do you mean Uncle Red?"

"He just arrived came home a few minutes ago. Where is he? His truck is parked in the garage."

A small black and white Papillion came running up to the

door. She was barking, but her tail was wagging and she appeared friendly.

"Quiet, Pickles. You don't want him to smack you again, do you?" the young man cautioned, picking up the small animal.

"Who hits him?" Jay asked, stepping up.

"Her, it's a her. Uncle Red. He hates that dog. She belonged to Ty before he died. We've been trying to find a home for Pickles but haven't had any luck," said the young man, shaking his head.

"Where is Uncle Red?" asked the Chief again.

"It was crazy. He came tearing up the stairs from the garage, grabbed the rent money off the table, and yelled we were on our own. He took off in a hurry out the back door."

"He wasn't here when we came to look over the house when Ty died," Nickerson observed.

"No, he came after Ty died. He said he was his uncle and he was going to stay for a while. We live down in the cellar. He stayed upstairs, but he really hated poor Pickles."

"He must have spotted you, Jay. He won't come back here now," the Chief commented.

"What about the dog?" the renter questioned, holding her.

"Let me see her," Jay said, reaching out for her.

She seemed friendly. Petite in size, her ears were bigger than her head and she had black freckles all over her white snout. The dog couldn't have weighed any more than nine pounds. She covered Jay's face with kisses and her white fluffy tail never stopped wagging.

"Are you sure she was Ty's dog?" Jay asked.

"He loved that dog. They were inseparable."

"What do you think, Chief? Should I take her?" Jay asked. "She'd be great company for Angie. I would be able to leave her at the house instead of keeping her in my office at work with me if she had a little companion at home."

Since Pickles had tags, they were able to determine that she was up to date on her shots. Ty had apparently taken good care of her. A second bone-shaped tag had the local vet's phone number and Ty's name and number. She had also been chipped.

"She's probably so confused. Ty hasn't come home and the dog just doesn't understand where he is," Jay observed, stroking her to calm her down.

"She sits in the window watching for Ty, whining. That's why Red would hit her, to shut her up. When we were home we would keep her downstairs with us. Pickles is a good dog and she deserves better. I'd keep her in a minute, but I have to return to Bulgaria in a few months," the young man stated.

"Is it okay if I take her?" Jay proposed. "I can guarantee that she'll have a good home and a new best friend named Angie."

"Ty's dead; I think the dog needs someone who will love her as much as he did. Let me get her bed and toys together for you."

"Nickerson, call for a tow truck to impound the suspect's vehicle. Stay down near the truck so he doesn't circle back and take off with it," Boyd ordered.

All Pickles' belongings were gathered up and put in a green trash bag. The renter petted the dog one last time and said goodbye. He thanked Jay for stepping up and helping out with the lonely puppy.

"She won't be lonely anymore," Jay promised, hugging the little dog close. "Chief, can I talk to you a minute before I leave?" The two men strolled outside to Jay's car.

"I know it's nothing you can use in court, but Roland told me Red was one of the guys who broke into my house last night," Jay confirmed. "He didn't see him, but he heard the second suspect calling him by name."

"Nickerson told me what happened. Your house was pretty trashed, huh?"

"Yea, I still haven't finished cleaning it up yet," Jay stated unhappily.

"Do you know what they were looking for?" the Chief questioned.

"I'm certain it was Roland's journal. I found it in the tunnel after you had left," Jay shared with him, secretly waiting to be yelled at for withholding evidence.

"Did they get it?" Boyd wondered out loud.

"No, I locked it in my safe along with the gold coin I found on the floor near the tunnel door."

"You found a gold coin?" his friend asked, momenttarily forgetting about the journal.

"Roland says it's part of the treasure," answered Jay. "He stated that it is a gold doubloon."

"I need to go inside and check this place out to see if I can figure out where Redmond went. And, Jay, when you're done with the journal, hand it over, okay? It is evidence in a murder case."

"I will," he assured the Chief. "Come on, Pickles. You have a new sister I want to introduce you to. I sure do hope you two can get along."

Pickles perched on the front seat staring at Jay. She tilted her head and when she did, her ear flopped over to the side. She was so cute and small, Jay figured she must have been the runt of the litter. They drove back to the cottage together where Robbie was sitting on the front porch with Angie still waiting for the glass repairman to arrive.

As the car stopped, Pickles scooted her front paws up on the dashboard to look out the front window. Both dogs spotted each other at exactly the same time. Angie ran up to the passenger's side of the car barking as Pickles was jumping up and down on the seat trying to see out the window.

"Robbie, can you take Angie inside?" Jay called out through the car window.

Jay picked up Pickles and hoped fervently that this wouldn't turn into a dog fight. He walked through the door and told Angie to sit and stay. He set Pickles on the floor and held on to her leash as Pickles' sniffed her way around the house. Angie sat, intently focused on the other dog. Pickles strained on the leash wanting to check out her new friend.

"Angie, be a good girl," Jay ordered.

The two dog's noses met, and Pickles' tail started wagging harder. She stuck her butt up in the air, her front paws flat on the floor like she was ready to play with her new roommate. Angie laid down, watching the smaller dog dancing around her. Pickles decided she wanted to explore the rest of the house when Jay let her off the leash. Angie, bored with the situation, sidled over to her bed and simply laid down, but kept her eyes trained on Pickles.

After finding the back door, the food and water dishes, along with several of Angie's toys, Pickles wandered over to Angie's bed, turned in a circle twice, and curled up next to her new friend. The golden looked at Jay like "Seriously?"

"Good girl, Angie. Looks like you have a new friend," Jay told her, walking over and patting them both at the same time. Angie sighed and laid her head down. Pickles snuggled up against her new friend and contently closed her eyes.

"And you were worried," said Robbie, smiling. "She's a real cutie. Where'd you find her?"

Jay explained where she came from and how he had ended up with her. As they were talking, the window repairman showed up to finally fix the front door. He stayed home put while Robbie went to check on the happenings at the café. Jay lazed on the floor near the dogs while the front door was open. He had clipped the leash back on Pickles just in case she tried to run out the door; she never even opened her eyes. It took fifteen minutes and the glass was finally repaired. As the handyman departed, Jay looked at the two dogs and grinned.

"Welcome home, Pickles."

Chapter 16

JAY STARTED TO clean up the trashed office. After an hour, he looked at his watch and realized it was lunch time and with the rain the café would be busy. He walked the dogs out on their leashes and let them do their thing before he marched them over to the café. Wanting to give them a little more time together before leaving them alone at the cottage, he took them to his office first. He wanted to determine if Pickles would bark and disturb the customers trying to enjoy their meals.

He had carried in the small dog bed with them and set it next to Angie's bed on the floor. Angie laid down on her bed, but the smaller dog didn't seem to want to sleep by herself. She finally just curled up on Angie's bed right next to the big dog. Jay flipped through the mail on his desk and saw they were mostly bills, so he decided to open them later.

"Be good girls," he instructed to the sleepy dogs as he closed the office door tight.

The place was hopping; a typical rainy day on Cape Cod. He helped Kathy seat people all the while keeping an ear out for the dogs. The sun broke through the darkened clouds around one-thirty. High tide was at three which meant it would be a late beach day that would translate into a late supper rush.

As things slowed down, Jay decided to take the girls out to pee. He strolled out the back door of the office, one leash on each hand. Four picnic tables had been set out behind the café for the employees to take their breaks and they were filled up. It was the first time anyone had met Pickles. They already loved

Angie and now Pickles was finally getting the attention she had craved for so long.

Susan, the executive chef, moved around to the other side of the picnic table.

"Don't you like dogs?" asked one of the waitresses in confusion.

"I'm allergic to dogs and cats," she explained sadly. "I love them, but they don't love me. That's why I never come into your office, Jay. I always have to send someone else in there."

"I didn't know that. The girls will be staying at the cottage once I know they can get along okay," Jay relayed. "I'll have the office cleaned so you can come talk to me if need be."

"Thanks. Well, back to work," Susan exclaimed, standing up.

Jay watched his executive chef walk away slowly. Why didn't Josh like her? He had said she tried too hard to be everyone's friend. Was that a cover so no one would suspect her of anything? Jay realized he needed to watch everyone and trust absolutely no one. He shook his head in disgust. If it hadn't been for this stupid treasure, his business and life would be running smoothly now. His mother wouldn't be in the hospital and his house wouldn't have been burglarized. He had to figure out who the inside person was. But, how? He had been away from the Cape too long to know the new wash-a-shores.

He settled back in the office, did some paperwork, and left the girls playing tug of war to go sit at the bar and have an early supper. Robbie was alone on the bar until five. Jay decided to order a scotch on the rocks. Robbie set the iced glass on the bar and as he turned to get the scotch bottle, Jay watched the glass slide down to the other end of the bar. He chuckled, knowing Roland was harassing his brother again. Robbie turned, mumbled something under his breath, and ambled over to get the glass.

"Why does he like to annoy me?" Robbie complained.

"Maybe, he didn't have a younger sibling growing up and he's making up for it with you," suggested Jay, smiling. "Or maybe, just because you do get annoyed."

"Great. I'm a ghost's stand-in," Robbie groused, placing the scotch bottle back on the shelf where it belonged. "Have you had a chance to look at the journal yet?"

"No. I'm off tomorrow. I'm going to the hospital in the morning and I am going to spend some time in my home office copying the journal pages. Boyd said he wants the journal ASAP. He wasn't nasty about it or anything, but he does want it back."

"It's funny," Robbie said, leaning on the bar in front of his brother. "Since the cameras were installed, it's been kind of quiet."

"I sure hope it stays that way," Jay reiterated, looking at the huge burger placed in front of him by one of his waitresses. "Thanks, Anna."

"I have to admit," Robbie confided. "I am kind of looking forward to exploring around the cellar some more. Finding that tunnel was so cool."

"Yes, I have to agree with you there. I just hope the journal tells us where the rest of the secret rooms and passages are. I don't know how many Red found before we discovered the journal. He could be hiding in any of them watching us."

"Dude, that's a creepy thought," Robbie reflected, refilling his brother's scotch glass.

As orders started coming in from the dining room for drinks, Jay sat there eating his supper trying to figure out who the inside person could be. He also remembered that he still had no one to cook chowder for his Mom's shifts yet. Mary had only had one day off since Martha went into the hospital. Who could he trust with the recipe?

The first person who popped into his mind was Josh. It would get him away from Susan and he would basically be working by himself in the morning. Jay made a note to himself to talk to him tomorrow.

The night was busy. After finally locking the door, Jay let the two dogs run free on the first floor. Pickles followed Angie everywhere she went, her tiny legs working triple time to keep up with her new friend. As Jay was closing out the register, a loud bang came from upstairs. Both dogs started barking frantically. Jay walked over to the bottom of the stairs and called up..

"Roland, is that you?" Jay yelled.

No answer. The dogs continued their racket.

"Angie, stay," ordered Jay, hoping Pickles would obey the same command.

He turned on all the lights upstairs. Walking around, he called Roland's name several times, receiving no answer. Three bottles on the bar shelf had been tipped over.

Do I have more ghosts?

He walked behind the bar. Nothing else looked out of place besides the bottles. Jay heard a small growl and looked down to see Pickles was staring at the wall behind the bar. Her tail was between her legs, her ears flat against her head, and she was showing her tiny teeth. Thinking Roland was around and the little dog hadn't met the ghost yet, he picked up Pickles and tried to calm her down.

She was still growling, but started quivering in fright at the same time. If it wasn't Roland, who was causing the tiny dog to act like this? Roland appeared at the end of the bar and Pickles immediately stopped growling.

She stared in the ghost's direction, not afraid of him at all.

"I had a feeling it was you who was spooking the dog," said Jay. "Meet Pickles."

Another one?

"Yes, she was Ty's dog. I followed Redmond to where he was staying and found out that he had been abusing this poor little dog since Ty died. There was no one else to take her in, so I did. She's a loveable dog and well trained."

Are they going to stay at my cottage?

"Yes, they will be staying at *my* cottage," Jay clarified. "Did you just tip over those bottles?"

Wasn't me...

"Do we have more ghosts in here than just you?" Jay asked in sudden dismay.

Maybe.

"Great. I guess I should finish closing up. Have a good night, my friend," Jay remarked, carrying the tiny dog downstairs with him.

Angie was sitting right where Jay had commanded her to stay. Her tail started wagging as she caught sight of him. Jay set Pickles onto the floor and hugged Angie, telling her what a good dog she was.

"I have a special treat for you when we get home," he promised Angie.

True to his word, he gave her a new soup bone to chew on when they returned to the cottage. Pickles was given a smaller version of Angie's. The dogs happily chewed on their new rewards while Jay sat on the back deck enjoying his after-work beer.

It was approaching twelve-twenty when he saw the three pirate ghosts walking the point again. It was the exact same time that he had seen them the other night. Tomorrow night, he would walk to the point and wait to see if they showed up when there was a living person in the area.

They must be a residual haunting, doing the same thing at the same time. Maybe, it was the last night they walked to the cave before the captain murdered them to guard the treasure.

Jay watched them until they disappeared once more. He finished his beer, planning in his head how he would get closer to them. The bedroom was still a mess. The couch was pulled out and Jay sat down on the edge while Angie jumped up and settled in her spot. Pickles' legs were too short to climb up on the bed so Jay picked her up and placed her on the blanket. She walked over to Angie and snuggled in next to her friend's belly.

They slept in later than Jay wanted to the next morning. He drank his coffee watching the dogs from the deck while they went out for their morning relief. Pickles stayed right next to Angie, never straying from her side. They were eating breakfast while Jay opened the safe and took the journal upstairs to the copier in his home office.

It took him longer than he had planned to copy the pages as he kept stopping to read what he copied. The hand-drawn maps showed many secret rooms and passages underneath the café and lighthouse. There were also tunnels that led to the various outbuildings and one that even lead out to the lower point.

The closer Jay studied the maps of the café building, the more upset he became. The maps showed a secret passage that led right up to the back wall of the bar. Had someone been in the passageway last night and opened the door thinking no one was around? Is that how the bottles had been tipped over?

Pickles hadn't growled once at Roland. However, she did stare at the wall behind the bar, baring her teeth and snarling.

Could Redmond have been back there and she sensed it?

He had abused her so of course she wouldn't like him. Since he had nowhere to live now, was he maybe living in one of the secret tunnels?

He stapled the copies together and went downstairs to put both the original and the copies back in the safe. It was nine-thirty and Josh would soon be coming into work. Jay needed to ask him if he wanted to change two of his shifts to become the chowder cook with Mary.

"Come on, girls. Let's go for a walk," Jay called to them, grabbing the two leashes.

The ambled around the café and started down the hill.

Pickles was holding her leash in her teeth trying to walk herself. Angie trudged along at her usual pace, stopping every now and then to sniff something out. As Josh was coming up the hill, Angie started pulling harder on her leash. Jay let her go and she ran straight over to Josh. Her tail wagged back and forth as the young man hugged her tight. They walked up the hill together to where Jay was patiently waiting.

"Hey, Pickles," Josh said, bending down to pat the little dog. "Hi, Mr. Hallett."

"Before you go into work, I have a favor to ask," said Jay.

"Anything, what's up?"

"My Mom is going to be in the hospital for a while longer and I need to train someone else to take a couple of her shifts so that Mary can have her two days off," he answered. "Would you be willing to change two of your shift hours and come in early on those days to make the chowder?"

"You're going to trust me with the chowder recipe?" the young chef asked in wonder.

"If you promise to never tell anyone the secret ingredients. My Mom would be devastated if her recipe got out," Jay declared. "Do you want the job?"

"I sure do. Thanks for trusting me," Josh affirmed.

"How's your Mom doing?"

"She had her last dose of chemo yesterday," he answered, the strain evident in his voice.

"Good thing you were home with her," Jay encouraged. "I bet that made it a little easier for her."

"Yea, I'm glad that the whole procedure is over. Now, we wait to see if it worked," Josh added hopefully. "She knows how tight money is right now and doesn't want me buying the medicine she needs."

"If you need any help getting her prescriptions, you be sure and let me know," Jay requested.

"I will, thanks."

"Be there at seven tomorrow morning and Mary will start your training," Jay instructed. "I'll be in at ten to see how things are going."

"Thanks, Mr. Hallett. Have a great day off," Josh called back, walking up the hill.

The threesome finished their walk by going all the way down to the main road, past the beach, and back up to the cottage. Halfway up the hill, Pickles pooped out and had to be carried by Jay. Angie kept going, excited to be outdoors and not locked up in the café office.

He wanted to talk to Robbie so they went by the cottage, but his surf board was gone from the deck. Jay wanted his brother to check the wall behind the bar to see if he could find the secret opening. No one would think twice about Robbie looking around on the shelves of bottles since he was the bar manager.

They strolled past Robbie's place out to the point. Jay wanted to find a place to sit tonight while waiting for the three pirate ghosts. A formation of three large boulders, right off the path would give him the covering he needed. He could peer out over the ocean while he waited.

Returning to the cottage, he gave the girls fresh water. Angie decided it was nap time as she had walked the entire distance of their jaunt. Pickles laid down just because Angie did.

He took the journal out of the safe and decided to work on his tan. He would sit on the beach and scan over the book one more time before taking it to the Chief. Placing the journal in a clear plastic bag to protect it from the sand and water, he grabbed a water bottle out of the refrigerator, and headed out towards the beach.

He walked by the parking lot that he owned where the town was collecting money for tourists to park and use his beach property. He vowed this would be the last year that happened. It was privately owned land now and the town had no right to be making a profit off his land. It would be a tough fight to get them to stop, but one he felt justified in pursuing. He realized that being an attorney would still come in handy now and then.

The front section of his beach was overcrowded as it usually was on a hot summer day. He walked further down, along the water's edge, the cool water swirling around his feet making him wish he had worn his swim trunks.

Checking the upper point as he walked, he was searching for Colleen to see if she was at her usual spot looking for her mother. The ghost probably stayed hidden away on busy days like this.

Two girls in tiny bikinis ran by him, splashing in the water. They stopped a few feet away and smiled and Jay smiled back. He loved being back on Cape Cod in the summertime.

Settling on a spot up near the cliffs, he sat down. He buried his feet in the cool sand and shifted his sunglasses to the top of his head. The shirt came off next so he could get some sun on his pale, well-built body. Jay took a slug of water from his bottle and stood it up in the sand next to him.

Taking the journal out of the bag, he opened it up to the first page. Along the inside cover, down in the corner near the binding, he noticed a slight elevation in the surface. He ran his fingers over the bump. Something was definitely under the glued paper that formed the front cover. As he started to carefully peel back the pasted paper, a shadow fell over the book. Jay looked up expecting to see Redmond but it was Chef Brian Stoker who stood in front of him.

"Brian," Jay exclaimed, surprised that the chef would come approach him after not showing up for his job. "Can I help you with something?"

"I was wondering why your secretary called me and told me that I wasn't needed before I had even started," he answered. "I didn't even get a chance to prove I could do the job I was hired for. Was there a specific reason I was told not to come to work for you?"

"My secretary called you?" asked Jay in confusion.

"Yes, she said I was no longer needed for the position and it had been filled by someone else," he confirmed.

"Brian, number one, I don't have a secretary. Number two, I thought you were a no-show," Jay responded in surprise.

"I would never do that, not show up I mean," said Brian. "I was told not to come, so I didn't. I figured you had your reasons. So then, who called me?"

"I don't know who contacted you, but I will find out. Do you still want the job?" Jay asked.

"I can't. When I got the call from your place, I went out that afternoon and got a job at CheCherene on Main Street. It's only for the summer, but I needed a job."

"Brian, I'm really sorry this happened; I can't explain why it did. If you need a job after Labor Day when CheCherene closes, come see me. I'll guarantee you a job right through the winter," Jay said, sticking out his hand.

"Thank you, Mr. Hallett," Brian said, shaking the extended hand. "I guess I'll see you in a few months."

Jay leaned back against the sand wall behind him, thinking. So it was a female who had called Brian. The first name that popped into Jay's head was Susan. It seemed the evidence was starting to pile up against her. The peanuts in her purse when Ty died of a peanut allergy, Josh saying she tried too hard to make everyone like her, and now a female making phone calls involving the kitchen staff positions were making her the number one suspect on being the inside person.

But, what did she have to gain? What was her connection to the treasure? Susan didn't fill the position to make the chowder. Jay had filled the position himself. None of this was making any sense.

Opening the journal, he went back to the task at hand, peeling back the glued paper. The browned paper was so fragile it was disintegrating instead of peeling away. As careful as he was, the whole inside page started to crumble apart. A small flat key was stuck to the cardboard, and behind the key was a folded piece of paper.

Jay removed the key peering closely at both sides for any kind of markings. It was a plain, silver key, only one inch in length. He pried open the folded piece of paper. Numbers and letters, in a single column, were written at the center of the page.

50 R
112 L
15 R
21 R
25 D

These numbers could be a safe combination, but what would the D stand for? Maybe, they're some kind of directions. But, where is the starting point and again, what does D stand for? This key is way too small for a treasure chest.

He put the key and the folded paper back into his pants pocket. These items were not going to be returned with the journal. Roland's written words kept his interest for another two hours. He checked the back inner cover to make sure nothing more was hidden inside the book.

Jay stood up to put his shirt on only to realize that he was now sunburned on his back. Tucking the corner of the shirt into his back pocket, it hung over his well-shaped butt as he started his walk back to the road. Shirtless, many women eyed him as he passed by. Several more approached him to see if he was busy that night. He had made a pact with himself to lay off the dating scene until his business was finally well established. He politely told the women he was spoken for and said goodbye, flashing that to die for smile of his.

He slipped into the back door of his office. Knowing, that

according to the health code, he couldn't go out into the café shirtless, he slid his muscle shirt on over his sunburned back. Stopping at the hostess station to check in with Kathy, he then went upstairs to chat with his brother. Pulling him aside, he explained what he needed Robbie to do in regards to the back wall of the bar.

Robbie was none too pleased to find out that someone may be watching him from behind the wall, but he agreed to search for the opening. Robbie told his brother that he was going to come to him anyway because he had noticed some things missing from the bar over the last few days. Bottles of beer would be gone from the bar cooler in the morning when the bartender knew that he had stocked it full before he left for the night.

Next, Jay decided to confront Susan to get her reaction to the information that he had received on the beach about the phone call to Brian. He entered the kitchen at a brisk pace.

Susan wasn't on the line and she wasn't in the kitchen office. He walked directly over to Josh.

"Do you know where Susan is?" Jay asked.

"She said it was slow so she was going down cellar to get some work done," answered Josh, plating meatloaf and mashed potatoes.

"Thanks," Jay replied. "Looks good."

Down cellar, huh?

While trying to make up his mind whether to go down cellar and check on his missing employee or go to his office and watch the monitors, Susan came up the stairs covered in dirt.

"Hi, boss," she said cheerfully when she saw him at the top of the stairs.

"What were you doing down there, you're all filthy?" asked Jay, thinking maybe she was in the dirt tunnels.

"Health inspector is coming Monday morning," she answered. "I was moving things around and making sure all food products were on shelves or pallets."

"Why didn't you have some of the guys do it?" he asked.

"I'm still trying to set up a system down there to making ordering easier. I'm tagging the shelves under the product so we can order by the barcode when something is low," she explained.

"Are you going to cook like that?" he asked, pointing to her dirty clothes.

"No, I'm off at five today. I was going to finish up paperwork in the office and head home. Why? Do you need me to stay?"

"No, everything is fine. I just didn't want you serving the food looking like that."

"I wouldn't do that. It's disgusting to even think about it," she said, surveying her filthy clothes.

"You look pretty laid back today. Nice sunburn you're sporting," she said. "That's going to be real sore by tonight."

"I know. I got distracted reading on the beach and lost track of the time," answered Jay.

"I sure hope the book was worth it," she said, smiling.

Jay decided he was going to test her a little further.

"It was. I have a journal that belonged to one of the lighthouse keepers that manned this place over a hundred years ago," Jay disclosed, fishing for a reaction.

No reaction; nothing.

"That would be interesting reading, to see how they ran the place back then versus now. Of course, it wasn't a café then and they had no television or modern day conveniences. It must have been a pretty solitary life working here," Susan observed.

"I agree," said Jay. "I'll let you get back to work. I have errands to run on my only day off."

Someone had been standing in the corner of the dish room listening to every word of their conversation. Turning to reach for something in the dish rack as Jay walked by, neither he nor Susan would know that someone had been eavesdropping.

Red was right, he still has the journal.

Jay returned to his office and viewed the last hour on the cellar monitor in fast forward mode; Susan had never left the stock area. She had been doing exactly what she claimed to be doing while down cellar. All the evidence pointed to her, but she was covering her tracks well.

The girls greeted him at the door when he finally returned home. He let them out the back door as he stood on the deck with a cold beer. Pickles tried her hardest to keep up with Angie, but her little legs just couldn't go fast enough. She did her thing and wandered back to the deck. Standing on her back legs, she begged Jay to pick her up. He sat down in the deck chair and she jumped right into his lap.

Pickles fell asleep in his lap while Angie appeared to be playing with Colleen the ghost. Jay had finally formulated a plan in his mind to catch whoever was coming out at night from behind the bar. He called his brother's cell and told him what he wanted to do. Robbie did not want to sit on the point and watch for the pirate ghosts, but he would go to the café and wait in hiding for the intruder. Real people he could deal with; ghosts not so much.

Jay also called Chief Boyd. He told him the plans for later that night and asked him if either he or Nickerson wanted to be there to arrest whoever was staying in the tunnels. Jay was almost positive it was Redmond Jules, the murder suspect in Bea Thomas' brutal death. The Chief agreed to meet Jay at his house at twelve forty-five that night.

With the plans firmed up, he called Angie into the house and fed the girls their supper. He locked the journal, key and folded paper into his safe. The sunburn was deep red and hurting now; it always got worse at night, his mother had told them when they were younger. Showering with cool water to take the sting out of the sunburn on his back, he dressed in loose clothing to head out to the hospital.

Jay spoke with his Mom's doctor before he went in to sit with her. They were gradually weaning her off the medicine that had kept her in the induced coma. The swelling was gone around her brain and thankfully it didn't look like there would be any permanent damage. Her body was taking its time to heal. When she finally woke up, they would move her out of ICU and into a regular room. The doctor said everything looked promising for a full recovery.

He sat next to his Mom's bed gently holding her hand. She looked so pale and weak; growing up, he had never seen her any other way than strong and fearless. He had never pictured his Mom growing older, but laying motionless in the bed, she looked aged. Why hadn't he noticed how many years had passed before now? Because, he was too selfish and interested in his own life he realized, he had been driven to get that law degree. He should have known better than to leave her after Dad died, but at least she still had Robbie.

He knew in his heart she was closer to Robbie, always had been. She defended him no matter what. Maybe that's why he had decided to leave Anchor Point. Jay tried so hard to excel at everything and his brother never exerted himself the least little bit; they were total opposites.

It didn't matter anymore. He and Robbie were talking again and their Mom was going to be all right. When she was released from the hospital, she would come home and stay with Jay. He had that small den on the first floor that he could easily turn into a bedroom for her. It would be her home until she decided to finally relocate to Florida.

"I'm so sorry, Mom," Jay said, tearing up looking at the white bandage that covered her head.

He laid his head on her hand and cried. Maybe it was the beer he had been drinking all day or maybe it had just hit him how much his Mother really did mean to him.

"She will never blame you, you know," said a voice from

the door way.

Jay looked up; Cindy was standing there. Even though she wasn't immediate family, Jay had insisted her name be put on the list of allowed visitors. His Mom loved Cindy like a daughter and they remained close even after she and Jay had gone their separate ways.

"It wasn't your fault. You had no way of knowing something like this would happen," she comforted. "Your mother knows that."

He wiped the tears from his face with the back of his hand as Cindy walked to his side and laid her hand on his shoulder. Jay flinched away at her touch.

"Oh, that's a nasty one," she cringed, moving his shirt aside to see the red skin underneath. "Have you got any aloe at home?"

"No, I hadn't thought about it," he answered. "I'll pick some up on the way home."

"And who's going to put it on your back? Stormy?"

"I guess I haven't seen you in a while. Her name is actually Angie and she belonged to Mr. Peterson before he was put in the assisted living facility up in Plymouth. His kids abandoned the poor dog and she wound up living at the lighthouse," Jay explained.

"How did you find that out?" she asked.

"Have you had dinner yet? I have a lot to catch you up on. I'm going ghost hunting after I eat; maybe you'd like to sit with me and we could wait for the ghosts together?" Jay suggested. "You also need to meet Pickles."

"I would love to, but what's a Pickles?" she asked, smiling.

"Come on, we'll grab dinner at the café, you can meet Pickles, and then we'll go sit and wait for the ghosts," Jay said, standing up.

"Sounds good to me," she responded cheerfully.

Jay leaned over to gently kiss his Mom's head.

"I'll be back tomorrow," he whispered. "I'm going to have dinner with Cindy."

He could have sworn a slight smile crossed his Mother's lips as he turned away.

Chapter 17

THE CAFÉ WAS busy: even being the owner didn't have perks on a busy summer night. Together, they had a drink while they waited for the table they had shared on opening night. Jay started to catch Cindy up on all that had occurred in the last couple of weeks. She had asked several times what a "Pickles" was, but Jay told her she would have to wait and see. They enjoyed a quiet dinner together looking out over the glassy ocean.

Steering back towards to the keepers' cottage, Jay noticed Roland standing watch up in the old lighthouse. Cindy saw him, too and waved, but Roland stood with his hands behind his back watching out over the ocean. They arrived at the cottage to the sound of loud barking from inside.

"That sounds like two different barks to me," Cindy noted.

Jay unlocked the front door with a flourish.

"Go ahead," he insisted with a huge grin. "Go see what a "Pickles" is."

Cindy opened the door to Angie jumping up on her to greet her. Pickles, not to be outdone, tried to jump up on her other leg but fell flat on her butt.

"Hello again, Angie," she said, patting the dog. "I know, I haven't seen you for a while. And goodness, who is your new friend?"

Cindy sat cross-legged on the floor with one arm around the golden as Pickles jumped into her lap. She was getting covered with kisses from both dogs. Laughing in pure joy, she laid back on the floor and let the excited dogs crawl all over her. Watching her with his dogs, Jay realized all at once that she was the one for him.

"How do you like Pickles?" he asked, laughing at the bath Cindy was getting with slobber.

"She's adorable!" she got out between the heartfelt dog kisses.

"Okay, girls, let Cindy up," Jay said, extending his hand to her.

He clasped the leashes on the dogs to take them out to perform their nightly business. Cindy grabbed Pickle's leash and Jay walked Angie. After they returned to the cottage, they opened a bottle of wine, and sat on the couch with the two dogs sleeping between them. Jay shared the story of how he had ended up with Pickles. They talked about how their businesses were doing during the tourist season and how their families were.

Cindy liberally spread aloe lotion on Jay's back twice to help with the burn. Besides the tingle of the aloe on the sunburn, Jay was experiencing other tingles of his own at Cindy's soft touch. He badly wanted to kiss her, but he restrained himself knowing that he was the one who had left her. He had no right to think things would simply go back to the way they had been just because he had come home to Anchor Point.

"Earth to Jay. Hello?" Cindy called to him, snapping him out of his thoughts.

"Sorry. Just thinking about old times," he answered honestly without realizing what he was saying.

"I do that a lot too," she answered quietly. "Especially since you came back home."

He turned and gazed into her eyes. She sucked in a breath and held it, afraid of what he would say. He hesitated; had he matured enough to face commitment this time around?

"Jay, why did you really leave Anchor Point?" she asked pointedly.

"I was afraid," was all he could manage to say.

"Afraid of what? Me? Commitment?" she asked in a puzzled voice. "I know you wanted your law degree and that cushy job in Boston, but you didn't even ask me to go with you. It made me think that you were running away from me."

"I guess looking back, I was running from us," he answered honestly.

"I knew it. Your mother knew it, too. She kept telling me to wait and you would eventually come home. She knew in her heart you would return to Anchor Point and to me. I never had the strong conviction that she did," Cindy offered up, sipping her wine. "You did come home to Anchor Point, Jay, but did you come home to me?"

"The entire time I lived in Boston, I knew that I had done the wrong thing. I dated many women, but across every dinner table all I saw was your face. Then I heard you got engaged. I stayed in Boston so I wouldn't have to face the fact that you were marrying someone else," Jay admitted.

"You never called or wrote to me, even when you first left."

"Originally, I was concentrating on getting my degree and passing the bar. It was a stressful time for me. Once I landed the job at the most prestigious law firm in Boston, I realized that I had absolutely no one to share my success with. Having the words 'attorney at law' after my name wasn't so important after all."

"Why didn't you call me?" she questioned.

"I told you, I thought you were engaged."

"What made you come home, truthfully?"

"I had a high-profile case representing a very wealthy man's son. He paid me well to look the other way while he and his family bought off the judge. In the process, a young girl was killed for refusing to take the bribe that was offered to her. She was going to testify against them because she told me it was the right thing to do. It was never proven who or why she was killed, but I know in my heart who had ordered her hit."

"That's awful. Rich people think they are above the law and that they can buy anything," said Cindy, refilling her glass. "So, what happened?"

"The firm ended up depositing large sums of money into my personal bank accounts. Five million dollars, to be exact. They told me if I went to the police, they would testify that I was crooked and got paid well for looking the other way. They insisted that if I didn't play along and let the matter drop, they would frame me instead for the woman's death."

"Why didn't you go to the police anyway?"

"Who do you think they would have believed? A firm of well-known attorneys who have practiced in Boston for over a hundred years teamed with a rich, high society family, or me, a young upstart attorney who hadn't been in practice for even three years? They knew what they were doing when they assigned me the case. I was their scapegoat if anything went wrong."

"I see your point," Cindy said, shaking her head sadly.

"I took the money out of all the accounts they had access to and returned to Anchor Point and bought this place. I knew it was blood money, but I figured if I could help some residents here keep year-round jobs, that I would be doing something good in her name."

"Will they come after you?"

"I informed them that they would never hear from me again. I also told them that I had incriminating papers that would be released upon my death if I died in any way other than natural causes. I have envelopes with duplicate contents at five different law offices spread out all over the country. They wouldn't dare try anything," Jay said grimly. "They agreed to terminate the work relationship; my name would be removed from their records as if I had never even worked there. So far, they have kept their word."

"Are you afraid of them?"

"Sometimes, I find myself looking over my shoulder. When this whole mess started with the treasure, I thought for sure it was the firm starting trouble for me. That's the reason why I haven't called you; I didn't want you to get involved in this whole mess. I was so afraid that they might hurt you to get to me."

"You can't just live your whole life in fear of them, Jay. You sound as if you have your bases fully covered. I'm not afraid. Do you really want to start dating again or is this just another excuse?"

"It's not an excuse. I would be devastated if anything happened to you because of me," he said firmly. "I love you, Cindy, I always have. That's one thing that will never change."

"I love you, too. That's why I couldn't get married last year. I only want to be married to you," she said softly.

"Someday," he said. "Someday, I promise."

She laid her head on Jay's shoulder and they sat in comfortable silence drinking their wine together.

"What time do we have to be out on the point?" Cindy asked. "It's almost midnight."

"We should go now. They usually walk down the path about twelve-twenty," answered Jay. "Do you need a sweatshirt? I have extras if you do."

They walked out to the point, hand in hand, to the spot Jay decided would have the best vantage point. Sitting down ten feet off the path in front of three large boulders, they had a perfect line of sight both ways along the path. It wasn't long before they saw what they had hoped to see.

The three ghosts dressed in clothes from the eighteen-hundreds, floated mistily towards them. The strange thing was, they weren't actually on the path, but walking over the side of the cliff in midair. They didn't even break stride when Jay stood up to get a better look at them; the living simply didn't exist in their world. They passed by him on their nightly walk to the cave without so much as a glance.

"Come on," Jay said, holding out his hand to Cindy. "Let's follow them and see where they go."

The couple trailed closely behind the floating threesome. The pirates' mouths were moving in conversation, but Jay and Cindy couldn't hear any words being spoken. Fifty feet further down the path, the pirates took a downward direction through the air and disappeared suddenly and were gone from sight. Jay marked the spot on the side of the path as to where the cave entrance must have been back then when the pirates were alive and the treasure was buried.

"That was awesome!" Cindy gushed in excitement.

"They must have been walking on the point where the land still existed back then. Now, it's nothing but air. The ocean sure has washed away an awful lot," Jay observed.

"They do this every night?" Cindy asked.

"I believe so," Jay answered. "We need to head back to the cottage. I am supposed to meet Boyd and Robbie in five minutes. We are heading back to the café to see if we can catch whoever is living in the secret tunnels. Personally, I think it's Redmond Jules."

"Do you want me to stay here with the dogs?" Cindy offered.

"We might end up staying there all night," Jay answered. "He obviously comes out and grabs food and beer, but we have no idea when. It might be better if you just head home."

They arrived shortly at the cottage where Chief Boyd and Robbie were already waiting.

"Did you see them?" Robbie asked.

"We sure did. It was unbelievable," answered Cindy. "We were only ten feet away from them."

"You guys are nuts. Chasing ghosts is just not a normal thing to do," Robbie declared.

"What about all the paranormal shows on television?" Cindy

observed. "Are they all crazy, too?"

"Yea, but they get paid to do it. You don't," he answered sarcastically.

"I really hate to break this up, but if we wait too much longer we might miss him sneaking around the café," Boyd interrupted.

"Yea, I locked up the place at eleven-thirty, so he's already had over an hour to roam around," Robbie commented.

Jay gave Cindy a kiss and told her he'd call her later. They headed to the café as Cindy drove down the hill. Entering the café from the loading dock entrance, they silently tread up the stairs and then spaced themselves out around the bar. Using their phones to communicate, they texted back and forth to keep silent.

Two-thirty rolled around and Robbie had dozed off on the floor to the left of the bar. Jay stood up to stretch his legs as a noise sounded from behind the bar. Jay signaled Boyd who rose to his feet and stood ready to tackle whoever exited the wall.

The section of the wall to the right of the liquor shelves swung open suddenly. A man dressed all in black, entered through the opening and went straight for the beer cooler. They waited breathlessly until he was bent over reaching in for a beer, and then they tackled him to the floor together, Jay from the right and Boyd from the left.

He didn't go down easy. Jay was screaming for Robbie to turn on the lights as the suspect bit Boyd and punched Jay in the face trying to get away. The lights flared on over the bar. Still battling to get the man down on the floor to handcuff him, Robbie slipped up from behind and hit him below the knees taking him down with the other two crashing down on top of him. He was handcuffed tightly and leaned up against the bar.

It wasn't Redmond Jules as expected; it was Gabe Fulton, the newspaper reporter who had written the story on the café opening and who had captured the picture of Roland.

"Gabe, what the hell?" Jay asked in surprise.

"Jay, you got him? I need to wash out this bite," Boyd grunted out, looking at the back of his marked hand.

"Robbie, let's help our newspaper reporter friend here to sit down on the floor," suggested Jay, pushing the intruder down the cooler. "How'd you know about the tunnels?"

Boyd returned with a clean bar towel wrapped around his injured hand. Gabe sat sulking on the floor, silent, refusing to answer any of their questions.

"You're facing a boatload of charges, Gabe. Breaking and entering, robbery, assaulting a police officer, trespassing, and murder," Boyd curtly informed him.

"Murder? I didn't kill anyone. I may have done everything else you named, but I didn't murder anybody," he insisted.

"The only way you could have possibly known about the tunnels is if you read Roland's journal, and Bea was murdered for that journal. If you had the book, then you must have killed Bea," reasoned Jay.

"I read the journal, but I didn't kill the old lady at the historical society," he mumbled.

"Then who did? Who killed Bea? Everything's pointing to you for her murder," the Chief declared. "You had better start telling me something that's going to clear you of the murder charge."

"Ty's Uncle Red killed Bea. I didn't, I swear."

"How do you know Ty and his uncle?" asked Boyd.

"Ty is my foster brother. When I saw the ghost in the picture at the café opening, I figured if the ghost was true than the treasure must also be true. I called Ty in Philly and talked him into coming back to apply for a job so we could nose around the place together."

"How did Red become involved in this?" Robbie wanted to know.

"Ty called him."

"Why?" Jay asked.

"His uncle got in touch with him several months before to tell him that he was related to him. In searching for the rest of his family, Red found out where Bea was living and that they were related to Roland Knowles. He hated his mother for deserting him when he was young. After she left, the father beat the crap out of Red and his sister every single day. He kept them locked up in the old cellar. He finally sent them to an orphanage and the first chance they got, they ran away and lived on the streets together until his sister became pregnant and she disappeared."

"How do you know all this?" asked Boyd.

"Ty told me. My parents had fostered him until he turned eighteen. Ty's Mom, Red's sister, was killed in an attempted robbery. He and his younger sister were placed into the foster care system and then he lost track of her. All I know is that her first name was Laura."

"Where is Red now?"

"I don't know. He was living at the house on Beach Road with Ty. But when Jay followed him home he decided he had to leave. I haven't seen him since," answered Gabe.

"Who hit my Mom in the cooler? Who is your inside contact that works here at my restaurant?" Jay demanded.

"I honestly don't know," Gabe cried out, burying his face in his hands. "It must be someone who's working with Red."

"It's probably the same person who killed your foster brother. Doesn't that piss you off?" Robbie interrogated. "Who killed Ty?"

"I don't know."

"You don't know or you won't tell?" Boyd wanted clarification.

"I don't know. No one was supposed to get hurt. We were only going to hunt for the treasure and nothing else."

"You're sure it was Red who killed Bea?" the Chief asked again.

"I was at the beach house when he came back with the journal and the other papers. He was covered in blood and it was all over the inside of his truck, too," said Gabe. "Ty asked him what'd he'd done. He told us he got even with the mother who had made his life so miserable. He said if either of us told anyone, we'd be next. Then he walked over to the outdoor shower and stood under the spray with his clothes on. Later that day, I heard about Bea being murdered and then I knew that's who Red had been talking about."

"We'll have to test the truck tomorrow for blood residue," Boyd stated. "Okay, let's go."

"All I wanted was to be rich; I just wanted to find the treasure. I didn't kill anyone, I swear," whined Gabe as the Chief dragged him out the door to the cruiser.

"Let's close up this door and go home and get some sleep," Jay suggested, looking at his watch.

"We still have no idea who killed Ty, who clocked Mom, or where Red is," Robbie vented.

Roland sadly watched the two brothers leave the café. The treasure that had killed him way back when was still causing problems over a hundred years later. Martha was right; she had said not to tell anyone that it was still here. He would keep anyone away who got close to it. Roland decided that night, no one else would die for his treasure.

Chapter 18

JAY AWAKENED SLOWLY around ten. He let the dogs out and brewed himself a cup of hot, dark coffee. He had given Kathy the safe combination so she could access the money to set up the cash register drawers if he wasn't there before opening. The girls scarfed down their breakfast and Jay headed for the café. Unfortunately, he always had a ton of paperwork to catch up on after his day off.

"Had some excitement here last night, I guess?" Kathy asked as he walked through the front door.

"Yea, but how did you know?" Jay questioned, puzzled that the word had gotten out so quickly.

"It came over the police scanner, which is usually quiet at three o'clock in the morning," she answered. "Did you catch whoever hurt your Mom?"

"We caught someone, but I don't think he had anything to do with my Mom's attack," Jay said. "Is the mail in my office?"

"On your desk," she answered, picking up the menus to seat customers that had just walked through the door.

Sorting through the mail, a large manila envelope at the bottom of pile caught his eye. It was addressed to Jay personally and not the business. It was from a law firm in Plymouth; Mr. Peterson's attorneys had sent Jay a copy of the will in which he was mentioned. An attached letter from the attorney requested his presence at the formal reading of the will. The children had already filed papers to fight the last will their father had executed. The reading was not going to be until September, well after Labor Day.

How do I get myself involved in these things? he pondered to himself.

He put the papers down and leaned back in his chair and heard a loud sigh behind him.

"Hello, Roland. Why the heavy sigh?" Jay asked, turning in his chair to face the ghost.

How's Martha?

"She's getting better every day," Jay answered in relief. "The doctors say she will make a full recovery."

Will she come back to work? I so enjoy our conversations.

"I hope so. She's going to stay at the cottage with me for a while when she gets out of the hospital. You are welcome to visit her there while I am at work."

You got him last night, the man who hurt Martha?

"No, he wasn't the one. There is still another person on staff who hurt my Mom and killed Ty. We haven't figured out who yet, but I am certain we will."

No one will ever get to the treasure, I will make sure of that. It will stay hidden forever.

"I'm still going to search for it in my spare time, Roland. I want to open that museum I told you about. I won't give up," Jay said, staring out the window.

Martha doesn't want it found.

"She'll help me when she realizes what I want to do with it. Don't you want people to see your tunnel dedicated to the lost souls of the wrecks? Don't you want people to know their names?" Jay asked.

That would be a good thing. Then maybe their souls could finally rest in peace.

"I'm going to find it, Roland. Someday I promise you, I'm going to find it," Jay stated, watching a figure cross the point heading to the outbuildings on his property.

He stood up and walked over closer to the window. A man

disappeared behind the building where the truck with the plow was kept and he didn't come back out the other side. Then, he suddenly saw the figure further down the hill heading towards the main road. He turned to Roland, but he had disappeared. Sitting down in the chair again, he closed his eyes and tried to think. And then, out of the blue, it hit him; the smallest clue he had somehow overlooked that gave away who the inside person was. He quickly dialed his cell phone.

"Chief, you need to come to the café. I know who the staff member is that's working with Red. Good, I'll meet you out front."

Boyd and Nickerson pulled up to the front of the café.

"Who is it, Jay?" Boyd demanded, stepping out of his cruiser.

"Come with me to the kitchen," Jay insisted, opening the front door to the café.

The three men stood together near the kitchen office. The staff was looking worried thinking that someone else had been hurt. Jay called Susan and Josh over to join them.

"What's up, boss?" Susan asked in puzzlement.

"Susan, you were being set up to take the fall," Jay started explaining. "Isn't that right, Josh?"

His eyes got big and he suddenly bolted for the back door. Nickerson was faster and stepped in front of him to block his escape. He grabbed Josh by the arm and dragged him back to the group. The kitchen staff had frozen in place and were stunned to see what was unfolding right in front of them.

"The whole incident in the cellar when you were tied up was an act. Who helped you with it, Red?" Jay asked indignantly.

Josh stood there, not uttering a word.

"If we hadn't found you, he was returning later to let you out, wasn't he? It was a great plan to throw suspicion off yourself and onto to someone else, namely Susan."

"How did you know it was Josh?" the Chief wanted to

know.

"Last week after Josh was tied up in the cellar, I told him to take the next two and a half days off with pay. While he was out, I followed Red home and ended up adopting Pickles. Everyone else at the cafe had met Pickles for the first time when I brought her home. But the day Josh returned to work, he came up the hill and greeted Pickles by name," explained Jay.

"And exactly how would he know the dog's name if he hadn't been to work for two days unless he had seen the dog somewhere else?" added Nickerson.

"Exactly. That's how I figured out that he must have been over to Ty's house and knew the dog from there. Josh was the insider who kept an eye on everything and reported back to Red," concluded Jay.

"Damn, stupid dog…" Josh mumbled under his breath.

"Why did you attack my Mother?" Jay demanded to know.

"You'd better start answering the questions, Josh. You're looking at some serious charges and things will go much better for you if you cooperate with us," the Chief informed him.

"Your Mom caught me looking over the gold pocket watch in the walk-in. She came at me demanding I give it to her. I panicked; I knew Red would kill me if I lost that watch. Since he killed his own mother I knew he wouldn't think twice about killing me," Josh confessed.

"Then what happened?" the Chief asked.

"I tried to get by her and bumped the bucket of chowder and spilled it all over the place. I slid in it and dropped the watch which rolled under one of the racks. Martha got down on her hands and knees trying to retrieve it. I couldn't let her get the watch so I reached for the rolling pin and hit her in the back of the head with it," he said, tearing up. "I really like Martha, but I was more scared of what Red would do to me."

"When did you drop the watch down cellar?" Jay questioned.

"I didn't; I went back later to get the watch out of the walk-in, but it was gone," said Josh. "Honest."

"Nickerson, cuff him and read him his rights. Book him for assault and battery and murder. We'll finish this interrogation down at the station on tape."

"Murder! I didn't murder anyone," Josh screamed in a panic.

"We're holding you for the murder of Ty Fenster," the Chief informed him.

"But I didn't murder Ty."

"You were on the schedule the day he died and had access to his chowder," said Boyd.

"I might have been here, but I didn't kill him. I saw who did it. She came in the back door when everyone else was busy. Ty brought his dinner into the office and placed it on the desk. When he went to the walk-in with the produce clipboard, she ran out of the corner behind the dish room and poured some kind of ground up dust in his chowder. She mixed it in with her finger and then ran out the loading dock door. I watched the whole thing from the prep room. I saw Ty gasping for air after he returned from the walk-in and ate some of the chowder. He stopped moving so I went in to check on him. He was dead so I took the gold watch."

"Why didn't you say anything until now?" asked Nickerson.

"Because I thought Red had something to do with it, no, I knew he had something to do with it and I'm afraid of him. So, I kept my mouth shut," Josh responded.

"Who is this person, this woman who killed him?" asked Boyd.

"Theresa Jules, Red's daughter, who he had given up for adoption after his wife left him because of his abuse," answered Josh staring at Mary Chase. "I'm not going to jail for something I didn't do."

All eyes turned to Mary who was standing there calmly

stirring the chowder.

"Mary Chase is Theresa Jules?" asked Jay in disbelief. "Quiet Mary Chase? She murdered her own cousin?"

Boyd walked over in her direction. She picked up a ladle of steaming hot chowder and threw it in the Chief's face and took off running. Susan unobtrusively stuck out her foot and tripped the chowder cook as she ran by. Sliding across the floor, she careened to a stop when she slammed into the wall.

"No one frames me for anything," Susan yelled, rolling up her sleeves, ready to fight.

Jay held onto Josh while Boyd and Nickerson picked Theresa Jules up off the floor and handcuffed her. She kicked and screamed like a banshee throughout the whole process.

"You... stupid... idiot. All you had to do was keep your mouth shut and we would have looked after your Mom. Now who's going to take care of her and pay for her medicine? You're an idiot just like Ty was," she screamed in pure rage.

"Ty loved my Mom; you and Red didn't. You love money and that stupid treasure more than family. The only reason I agreed to help you is because Ty said he would give me half his share to buy my Mom's medicine and keep her comfortable," Josh yelled back at her.

"Why would Ty promise something like that, Josh?" asked Jay.

"Because my Mom was his sister, Laura. He tried to find her for a long time and when he finally did, she was stricken with cancer. That's why he promised half of his share to my Mom," Josh explained.

"And you believed him?" shrieked Theresa. "You are an absolute idiot!"

"Why did you kill Ty?" Boyd asked Theresa.

No answer.

"Because Ty was going to the police to turn Red in for killing Bea Thomas," said Josh. "He couldn't live with the guilt of knowing who had killed his grandmother. He hated Red for what he did to Bea."

"Where is Red?" asked Boyd.

"He's hiding in the outbuildings located here on the property," Josh replied.

"Shut up, you moron. He'll kill you when he gets a chance," screamed Theresa.

"He won't get that chance from prison, now will he?" said Nickerson, dragging Theresa out the loading dock door, screaming the whole time.

"Come on, Josh, you're next," said Boyd. "Jay, I'll talk to you later."

"Back to work everyone," said Susan. "Nothing more to see here."

"Susan, I don't know what I can say to apologize to you for thinking you were the cause of all this," Jay stated sorrowfully.

"I can't believe quiet Mary was the one who murdered Ty. I've never heard her say more than two words. What an actress she was," Susan said, shaking her head in disbelief.

"It looks like I need two chowder cooks now instead of one," Jay observed. "We'd better get those pots off the stove before it's burnt and we have no chowder to serve at all."

"Right behind you, boss," Susan acknowledged with a smile.

Chapter 19

THAT NIGHT, REDMOND Jules was apprehended as he was returning to the plow building to hide out. He was arrested for the brutal murder of Bea Thomas. Jay and Robbie watched from the cottage back deck as they shoved him into the cruiser and took him away. They clinked their beer bottles together, toasting to the end of the trouble that had plagued the café since opening day.

"I still wish I had been there to see Mary screaming," Robbie said.

"You mean Theresa," Jay corrected.

"I knew her in summer camp. She was a lot older than me, but even at camp she was quiet and got picked on a lot."

"It will be interesting to see why she teamed up with her father after he ditched her way back when," Jay said. "I guess it all came down to the treasure and getting rich quick."

"What are you going to do about Josh?" Robbie wanted to know.

"I don't know; I have to wait to talk to Mom to see if she wants to press charges. The kid was scared for his life. I think I would have acted the same way if I was in his shoes," Jay said. "I think his Mom being sick and all he has done to take care of her has to count for something in the end."

"He seems like a good kid. I think he just got mixed up in with the wrong company, but for the right reasons," Robbie replied, grabbing another beer.

"I'm going to the hospital in the morning to tell Mom what

has happened. The doctor confirmed that she can hear everything we say to her. It's time she finally heard some good news for a change," Jay commented.

"I'm catching a few waves in the morning, but I'll be there in time to sit and have lunch with her since I don't work until five. See you then," Robbie confided, jumping down off the deck.

"Dude, you spilled the beer; what a waste," Jay chastised, using his brother's favorite word.

"Later," Robbie replied, smiling.

Jay stepped into the den, the dogs scampering close behind. He had figured out the room would hold a single bed, a night table, a good-size bureau, and a reading chair. Tomorrow he would order the furniture so the room would be ready for her when his Mom could come home. The dogs would be ecstatic to have the company during the day.

The next morning, Jay decided to let Pickles out without being attached to the runner. He had been working with her, teaching her commands and now was the time to see how much she had learned. She traipsed behind Angie everywhere, but did come back to the deck when her master called her. Jay gave her a big hug in approval.

"You're really my dog now, Pickles. You, me, and Angie; what a wonderful family we make!" Jay affirmed laughing at her antics. "Come on, Angie, time for breakfast."

Driving to the hospital, Jay was flagged down on Main Street by Chief Boyd. He informed Jay that Red was wanted in three other states on various charges including another murder charge. They were fighting to keep him here because of the severity of the crime against Bea. Chief Boyd reminded Jay that he still needed the journal as evidence, but told him he would return it to him after the trial. Jay thanked his friend and invited him to supper at the café that night, on the house.

As he stepped off the elevator at the ICU floor, Cindy was

standing at the nurse's station sobbing. Jay ran over to Cindy, almost knocking over a food cart in the process.

"Cindy, why are you crying? Has something happened to my Mom?" Jay asked, panicking.

"Mr. Hallett, please come with me," instructed one of the nurses.

Jay left Cindy behind and followed the nurse to his Mom's room. She stepped aside and he looked in the door, his Mom was sitting up and talking to the doctor. Jay felt tears sliding down his cheeks.

"Jay," ordered his Mom. "Stop that crying and come give me a hug."

He almost tripped over his own feet trying to get to her. He hugged her tightly and wouldn't let go for a long minute. The doctor excused himself saying he would be back later to check on Martha. Jay sat on the side of the bed squeezing his Mom's hand.

"We were so worried about you," Jay confessed through the tears.

"You don't think a whack on the head is going to finish off this tough old broad, do you?"

"It wasn't just a whack on the head, Mom. You had a fractured skull and a swollen brain," her son replied. "It was bad, really bad."

"Well, it's in the past now. Doc says I can thankfully get out of here in a few days."

"I am setting up the den as a bedroom for you at the cottage. You don't have to stay there forever, but at least until you get stronger and can go back to living on your own," insisted Jay. "Or, you can stay there until you go to Florida."

"About that," his Mom answered with a smile. "How would you like a permanent chowder cook? Theresa doesn't want to move to Florida now and leave her daughter and grandchildren."

"Seriously? You're going to stay on Anchor Point?"

"Yes, but I have to do something about finding a permanent place to live now that I have sold the house," she said.

"How would you like a cottage built on the lighthouse property just for you?" Jay asked. "There's plenty of room to build and you can pick where you want the cottage constructed."

"Is this a way to ease your conscious because of what happened to me?" his Mom asked. "It wasn't in any way your fault, Jay."

"Yes, I feel guilty, but no, it's not for that reason. I just figured you could have your own place to stay, no mortgage to worry about, and you could keep your job as head chowder cook."

"It does sound tempting," agreed Martha. "I will have to think about it. Is Roland still around? I do so enjoy that ghost and our conversations together."

"He asks about you every single day. You know, you can stay with me in the keeper's cottage until your place is built."

"Mom, I have to ask you something. Why did you draw a "T" in the spilt chowder on the walk-in floor? What did it stand for?" Jay inquired.

"It wasn't supposed to be a "T". It was supposed to be a "J", but I didn't have time to draw the little tail on the bottom before I passed out," Martha explained.

"Is it okay to come in?" Cindy requested from the door. "I called Robbie like you asked me to, Martha. I left him a message since he didn't answer his phone."

"He's out surfing," Jay commented. "He is coming to sit with you at lunch time."

"Some things never change," Martha smiled. "And some things do."

"We have so much to tell you, Mom," Jay confessed, reaching out for Cindy's hand.

"I know you do. Cindy and I had quite a conversation this morning," Martha remarked, beaming. "I knew you would come home, Jay; I felt it in my heart. And, I knew from the start that you two were meant to be together. Cindy knew it, that's why she never married what's his name. We just had to wait for you to catch up."

"Martha, I have to get back to work. I'll see you later, okay?" Cindy said, squeezing her hand.

"No more Martha, call me Mom," she said joyfully, smiling at her eldest son.

THE END

RECIPES

MARDI GRAS HOT CRAB DIP

Submitted by Tim Daniel

1/2 of an 8-ounce block of cream cheese
1/4 cup sour cream
1 teaspoon Worcester sauce
1/2 teaspoon dry mustard
1/8 teaspoon seafood seasoning
1/8 teaspoon garlic powder
1 drop Tabasco sauce
3 green onions chopped (divided)
1 can crabmeat drained
3/4 cup shredded cheese

Beat first 7 ingredients with mixer until creamy.
Reserve 1 teaspoon of green onions, set aside. Add remaining green onions, crabmeat, shredded cheese to the cream cheese mixture. Microwave on High 3 minutes. Stir after 1 1/2 minutes. Top with the remaining onions and some more cheese. Serve hot with crackers or bread rounds.

EASY CAJUN SEAFOOD STEW

Submitted by Melissa Kay Clarke

1 pound Cajun sausage cut in bite size pieces
1-2 pound shelled and deveined medium shrimp
2 cans crab meat drained
2 cans tiny shrimp drained
1 pound fresh fish cut in bite size pieces
1 1/2 cup instant rice
1 large can Rotel style tomatoes with green chilies
1 bag seasonings blend (in the freezer section - onions, peppers chopped)
1 Tablespoon oil
6 cups chicken stock

Optional - lump crab meat, cooked crawfish, cooked oysters or any other seafood you like

In a Dutch oven or other large pot, brown sausage and seasonings mix in oil. Add Rotel tomatoes and stock. Bring to a boil. Add fish and reduce to a simmer for 10 minutes. Turn off heat, add remaining items including instant rice. Stir. Cover and let sit 5 minutes. Serve.

I like a nice crispy garlic toast with mine.

KATHY'S CORN and HAMBURGER CHOWDER

Submitted by Kathy Julin

6 Medium potatoes, peeled and cut into bite-sized pieces
1 pound hamburger
4 to 5 cans of cream style corn
1 can evaporated milk
1 to 2 tablespoons sugar

Brown hamburger, set aside. Cook potatoes in a large pan, covered with water, boil until tender. DO NOT empty water.
Add cans of corn, can of evaporated milk, and hamburger.
Stir and simmer until heated through.
Add sugar to taste.
YUMMY!

GRANNY'S FISH CHOWDER

Submitted by Cathy MacKenzie

Sauté:
2 or 3 chopped onions
2 chopped celery stocks
in 4 tbsp. butter

Combine in large pot:
6 cups of water
2 or 3 potatoes, cut into small cubes
Sautéed onions and celery
2 vegetable bouillon cubes
Sprinkles of salt, pepper, tarragon, parsley, celery salt, paprika
1 bay leaf
3 whole cloves

Bring the above ingredients to a boil, reduce heat, and simmer 20-30 minutes until potatoes are tender. Remove the bay leaf and cloves.

Add to the water:
Fish, as desired, but at least 2 pounds
(small chunks of haddock fillets.)
Boil and then simmer until fish is cooked.
Sprinkle with flour (to thicken as desired) and stir into the liquid.
Add 1 cup of milk/milk blend/heavy cream
Simmer (do not boil) until piping hot.
Ladle into large bowls. Add a dollop of butter.
Sprinkle with paprika, parsley, and pepper.

DEATH BY CHOWDAH

Optional add-ins: shelled shrimp, lobster pieces, small scallops, mussels (steamed and shelled) (or pre-packaged fish chowder mixture and add additional shrimp, scallops, and lobster pieces as desired)

Serve with piping hot biscuits.

COOL CUCUMBER SALAD

Submitted by Donna Walo Clancy

2 large cucumbers, peeled and diced
2 large tomatoes, diced
1 small sweet onion, peeled and sliced
1 small green pepper, cored and diced
¼ cup sugar
½ cup vinegar
1 cup water
¼ cup vegetable oil
Salt and pepper

Combine sugar, vinegar, water, and oil together, mix well. Combine cucumbers, tomatoes, pepper, and onion in a bowl and pour dressing over them. Mix and chill.
Salt and pepper to taste.
Serves 6.
Good side dish in the summer.

SCALLOPS PRIMAVERA

Submitted by Betty Studley

1 pound bay scallops or sea scallops cut in ¼'s
2 garlic cloves
2 Tablespoons butter
2 scallions
½ cup white wine
½ cup olive oil
Angel Hair pasta, cooked and set aside
Steamed vegetables of your choice (optional)

Sauté scallions and garlic in butter. Add wine and olive oil, heat until hot. Toss in scallops and cook for approximately 5 minutes. Mix in steamed vegetables of choice (optional) and toss with pasta.
Serve with salad and Italian bread.

Made in the USA
Middletown, DE
25 May 2017